LETHAL ENGAGEMENT

AN UNBOUNDED NOVELLA

Books by Teyla Branton

Unbounded Novels
The Change
The Cure
The Escape
The Reckoning

Unbounded Novellas
Ava's Revenge
Mortal Brother
Lethal Engagement

Under the Name Rachel Branton
Tell Me No Lies
Your Eyes Don't Lie

LETHAL ENGAGEMENT

AN UNBOUNDED NOVELLA

TEYLA BRANTON

WHITE
STAR
PRESS

Lethal Engagement (An Unbounded Novella)

Published by White Star Press
P.O. Box 353
American Fork, Utah 84003

Printed in the United States of America
ISBN: 978-1-939203-61-8
Year of first printing: 2015

To my friend Andrea Pearson,
who has been a constant supporter.

CHAPTER 1

THE *IN BETWEEN* WAS NEITHER WARM NOR COLD, AND I DIDN'T experience the confusion or discomfort shifters had reported in past centuries. If anything, I felt hyperaware and secure. I was supposedly nowhere, but I had to be somewhere. Or perhaps I ceased to exist in the nanosecond it took me to shift from one place to the next.

There was no color in the *in between,* but numbers spun through my head, logical and safe. Numbers didn't lie. They didn't pretend to love you and then give you up to be murdered.

Finishing the shift, I appeared in the conference room located on the main floor of our San Diego Fortress. Those already in the conference room looked in my direction as I appeared, and I knew it was because of the soft *pop* and slight suction of air that accompanied my shifts. Ava O'Hare, the leader of our Renegade cell, was seated in her usual place at the head of the conference table. Dimitri Sidorov, our healer and second-in-command, was also present and seated on Ava's right. My fifth great-aunt Stella sat next to him. No one else had yet arrived.

Stella smiled and glanced my way, her neural headset blinking like an electric crown as she continued to work. She was half Japanese and half Irish, the most beautiful woman I'd ever met, even if that was partly because of the nanites she, as a technopath, controlled in her body.

Despite her smile, I saw the worry in her eyes, and something inside me stirred. When Stella looked at me that way, excitement lurked in my immediate future. And excitement in our line of business always meant trouble.

My gaze returned to Ava O'Hare. Since yesterday, she'd been holed up in this conference room with some of the others, namely Dimitri and Stella, and also Ritter, who was our ops leader. Now it appeared that whatever plans they'd been hatching involved me. I was more than ready. The past months of doing nothing here in this mansion-turned-Fortress while the world clamored for our blood had me on edge.

I started toward my customary seat beside Stella, but Ava indicated the chair to her left. I glanced at Stella again, for the first time experiencing a bit of unease. Perhaps we weren't waiting for the rest of our cell. Maybe I was the only one invited.

"Thank you for coming, Mari," Ava began, almost formally.

I could read nothing in her gray eyes, unyielding as steel. She looked as calm as ever, from her smooth blond hair to the crisp black suit. "Did something happen to the president?" I asked. "Or his son?"

Two months had passed since the president had announced the existence of the Unbounded to the world, a declaration forced upon him by our near-fatal prevention of an Emporium plan to embroil the world in nuclear warfare. Since then, we Unbounded Renegades had waited to see which way public opinion would swing and if the president would be able to enact laws to safeguard humanity. Not from Renegades, sworn to protect all humans, but from the Emporium Unbounded, our enemy, who believed they should rule over mortals as they would cattle.

"A situation is threatening our future," Ava said, "and we're hoping you can help."

"Hunters?" I plastered on a smile to hide the helpless rage that came with my question. Hunters were a group of people originally descended from Emporium Unbounded, and their sole purpose was to eliminate all Unbounded, regardless of their loyalties. But I had a better reason to hate them.

"Yes and no," Ava said.

As she spoke, Keene McIntyre and Cort Bagley came into the room, their gait hurried. Relief waved through me that I wasn't the only one on today's agenda. The half brothers were an integral part of our Renegade cell and apparently part of this upcoming op—whatever it was.

Keene sat next to me, and I purposely didn't meet his eyes. He'd been different since the fire in Venezuela when we'd been sent to gather intel, and I didn't know him well enough to pinpoint why. We'd survived, and he joked around with me like before, but it wasn't the same between us. Maybe because as one of the few mortal Renegades he'd been in real danger there, no matter how good he was in combat. I knew too well that facing death could change you. But he'd been fighting this battle for years, so what was different about Venezuela?

Cort nodded at me as he passed my chair and settled next to Keene. He would have been nerdy if he hadn't been Unbounded; instead, he was arresting in a scientific sort of way, with startling blue eyes that radiated intelligence. He'd lived half a millennium, but his physical age was closer to forty. I was too old for crushes, but if I hadn't been, he would be a good choice.

"I'm sure it can't help our situation that Hunters are spreading rumors about Unbounded having abilities," I said. "Makes it harder for everyone to accept us."

"Rumors?" Keene's eyes riveted on my face as he settled further into his high-backed leather chair, their disquieting green capturing mine against my will. His brown hair had grown several inches and added carelessness to his narrow face, currently shadowed by several days' beard growth. His long-sleeved T-shirt did nothing to hide his leanness or the corded muscles running along his arms. "Mortals are going to find out the truth about the abilities eventually." He spat the word *mortal* as if mocking the rest of us.

"Great. Then they'll be at our throats just like the Hunters." I matched his mocking tone.

Cort peered around his brother to address me. "Maybe things have to get worse before they get better, but we'll need to tell the mortals everything if we're going to work with them and plan a future together."

"I agree." Keene shifted his gaze to include Ava and the others. "We need everyone working together to beat the Emporium—and all those greedy politicians lining up to court them. It's time humanity contributed to their own protection."

He was right, of course, but I also wanted the Hunters to pay. To pay for what they'd done to our Renegade Unbounded, for how they were influencing the other mortals.

For what Trevor had done to me.

Swallowing hard, I pushed the thoughts away, especially the memories of Trevor staring up with vacant, unseeing eyes. My hand went instinctively to the knife strapped to my inner forearm under my sleeve. I wore a matching one on the other side, the knives an extension of me now. The Hunters would never see me coming.

Keene grinned, his eyes tracking my movements knowingly, and I couldn't help but grin back. The moment made me feel close to him like in Venezuela when we'd hidden from the Emporium. If those agents hadn't started the fire, maybe things would be different between us now. But the fire had happened, had raged quickly, almost unnaturally, out of control. I could have shifted out, of course, but I hadn't wanted to leave Keene. Together we'd managed to hide and finally escape.

I'd wanted to talk to Keene about what happened that day, but whenever he'd been here at the Fortress during the past two months, we were either with others or he'd shut himself inside Cort's office. I had no idea what the brothers were working on.

"We'll have time to deal with rumors later," Dimitri said, speaking for the first time. His words slid over me like a balm to my nerves. That was Dimitri, the calmest, most reasonable, and wisest member of our cell, perhaps because he'd lived a thousand years. The healer was also able to kill or heal with a touch. The short, broad man had once saved my life, and I loved him like the father I'd never known.

As Dimitri said, time was on our side. Unbounded aged two years for every hundred they lived. Most of us underwent the Change around thirty or thirty-one, but a few Changed at twenty-eight, like Stella, and others as late as thirty-five. As Unbounded, our life span was about two thousand years—if the Emporium or the Hunters didn't kill us first. Even with that happy little cloud hanging over me, I was amazed that I, Mari Jorgenson, former boring accountant, was now a semi-immortal Unbounded shifter. No way would I ever choose to go back.

Not to remove the target from my back.

Not even for Trevor.

"The Emporium is our real enemy. Don't ever forget that," Ava said almost absently. "Now, as you may have surmised, we have a mission for you, and it's of the utmost importance. President Mann has had his hands full dealing with the announcement he was forced to make regarding our existence. It's been rather ugly, helped along, as Mari mentioned, by our old friends the Hunters." She nodded at Stella, and a holographic image appeared over the table, the increased blinking on Stella's headset the only sign that she was controlling it. As a technopath, Stella could use her headset to connect with multiple computers at once, internalizing and processing more information in a few minutes than a roomful of pencil pushers on a computer network.

I stared, fascinated at the scene that appeared more realistic than looking out a window. Stella had recently installed the new technology, and this was my first real look at it. This holo presented a public rally featuring Hunters, who were once again preaching their gospel of hate and racism. Sound came through the conference room speakers as a man yelled, spittle flying from his mouth with his zeal. He claimed Unbounded were evil and had to be stopped before their progeny contaminated the entire world. The crowd cheered. When he proceeded to detail how to dismember Unbounded so they would remain dead, the roar of approval grew to a wild crescendo.

Abruptly, the sound died, disappearing with the image. "Hunters publicizing how to permanently kill Unbounded complicates things on many levels," Ava said, "especially where the president's Unbounded son is concerned." She nodded again at Stella, and a new hologram appeared.

More shouting and confusion resounded through the speakers embedded in the walls. Women, young and old, clogged the sidewalks and streets for miles outside the White House chanting, "Give us babies! We want Unbounded babies!" They carried signs that read *I Will Carry Your Unbounded Baby* and *My Ancestors Were Unbounded, My Child Might Be Too—Choose Me.* And, *Willing to Sleep with Any Unbounded.* The variations went on, each more bizarre than the last.

"Wait," I said. "Are they out there for Patrick Mann?" Patrick was the president's grown son. Or, more aptly, the president's adopted son, who the Emporium had planted as a baby and tried to turn against the president. Patrick's refusal to succumb, even after a year in a squalid prison, ranked him way up there on my list of people to admire.

Ava gestured for Stella to kill the sound. "That's right. They're all volunteering to bear his child."

Keene laughed. "Who would have guessed that would be a problem when he became the face of the Unbounded."

"It's every man's dream, isn't it?" I said, laughing with Keene. "A horde of adoring women. But I bet Patrick's not happy about it. My impression of him was that he's rather conservative."

A smile teased Ava's face. "Whatever his feelings on the matter, it's making his security rather difficult. There have been two serious attempts on his life. The first was a shot from a crowd outside the White House that killed a Secret Service agent. A man with Hunter affiliation was arrested. The attempt last week was by an eighteen-year-old woman, and it resulted in her death." Before Ava finished speaking, a picture of a young blonde took the place of the chanting women.

"Her name was Annabella Fredricks," Ava continued, "Somehow she got into the White House where she was found naked in Patrick's bed. He wasn't home, but Secret Service found her while doing their regular rounds, and she jumped off a balcony trying to get away. They've kept it from the media so far, but she had a knife on her."

I decided not to ask where she'd kept it.

"Someone on the staff had to let her in," Stella said, making the image disappear, "but they really don't know who."

Ava nodded. "Patrick has moved to a different location in DC with a smaller, handpicked staff, but there are no guarantees that it won't happen again. Or something like it."

Cort cleared his throat, a habit he often used before saying something unpleasant. "He can't go back into hiding in Europe. We need him out there talking to people. He's the only way we'll get the support of the people and restore sanity to the government. We need him to show that we're normal." Catching Keene's stare, he added, "I mean, normal in every way that counts."

Keene usually took the bait on something like that, especially from his brother, but this time he didn't respond. When I cocked a teasing brow at him, he only gave me a wistful smile. My stomach did an odd little flop, and for no reason at all, I recalled that closet in Venezuela when we'd been crammed in so tightly that his heart had beat out a pattern with mine.

It was a relief when Ava began speaking again. "We do need Patrick, and that's where this op comes in. Patrick needs a fiancée."

I couldn't help laughing at that. "You mean to get rid of all those women?" I motioned to where the holographs had been.

"I thought we'd advised him *not* to reconnect with the woman he was dating before he was abducted," Cort said. "I distinctly remember someone explaining the danger he'd be to her."

Ava shrugged. "Since when do the young ever listen?"

A chuckle ran through the conference room, all except for Keene and me, who were, of course, babies compared to the other three. He caught my gaze again and winked. I knew he was thinking that Unbounded sometimes took themselves far too seriously. I thought that all the time, and I *was* Unbounded.

"Well, the world is changing," Ava said. "We hope

that soon we'll no longer have to abandon our families for their safety. But, yes, Patrick did hook back up with his girlfriend, and things are going well enough between them that if he had his way, he'd be announcing his real engagement." Her gravestone eyes rested on me. "However, his girlfriend isn't going to work for us, and that's where you come in, Mari. We want you to pose as Patrick's fiancée until the threat is over."

"Why me if he practically has a fiancée already? We could just go in as bodyguards."

"First, the girlfriend won't agree to her engagement, at least not publicly." Stella adjusted her neural headset with one hand, giving me a brief glimpse of the tiny metal wires that nestled against her scalp and provided the connection between her brain and her computer network. "Lucinda Ririe puts a whole new spin on the word shy. Truthfully, it might have been every bit as much for her as for himself that Patrick gave up politics when he Changed. Being a technopath just gave him a way to leave successfully. But Lucinda—Luce for short—isn't ready for that kind of attention. At least not yet."

I understood only too well. In my old life any kind of attention that didn't involve numbers made me blush and shy away from people. But I wasn't like that anymore, and those days mostly seemed foggy and unreal. Now I felt strong and alive. Awake. Changed.

"Besides," Keene drawled, "I bet she doesn't have your fascination with knives."

"Exactly," Ava said. "Lucinda can't defend him the

way you can. At any rate, the Secret Service wouldn't be pleased to have us send in bodyguards—that's the job they're supposed to be doing. As Patrick's fiancée, you can accompany him everywhere and keep an eye out for any threat, especially internal ones. Your unique ability gives you the advantage in just about every encounter Stella has simulated."

She had a point there. Short of a special, electrically-generated containment field, nothing could keep me from shifting.

"Since we know you're in the Hunter database as an Unbounded descendent," Ava continued, "and we can't be sure we've eliminated or altered every photograph there might be of you online, you'll have to go in disguise and use a fake name. Stella has already created your new identity and begun posting photographs of you in various places where Patrick has been. The media will soon find them. You'll become an overnight sensation."

I grinned. "New identity, cameras flashing, cute guy to romance. Sounds great! When do I start? But can I drive a Jaguar? Gotta keep up appearances if I'm dating the president's son, don't I?"

"Oh, really?" Keene rolled his eyes. "Is that all it takes? A new identity and a car? What about a Ferrari? Would you go out with a guy just because he had a Ferrari?"

I leaned over and elbowed him. "Only if he's really hot. Otherwise, I'll save up and buy my own." We received good pay for our ops, aside from our regular stipend allotted us at our Change, so I wasn't just talking.

Ava's next words wiped the smile from my face. "I want you to understand that your life will be in danger every minute. We know the Emporium has plans to take over the country despite everything we are doing to stop them, and Patrick may be a part of their long term goals. If we don't learn what they're up to, this war to save humanity may be lost before it's truly begun."

CHAPTER 2

HER WORDS SHUDDERED THROUGH ME, AND FOR THE FIRST time, I felt inadequate. Why were they sending me? I wasn't the best fighter among the non-combat-gifted Unbounded. I couldn't sense thoughts like Ava and her descendent Erin, who was usually her first choice for ops like this. Yes, I could add pages of numbers with a single glance, but I couldn't manipulate other data anywhere as fast as Stella. I couldn't heal someone who was ill like Dimitri could, or whip up one of Cort's scientific solutions.

I got along with people. I could make them laugh. I always knew the time down to the second, and I could shift anywhere I'd visited before, or someplace Erin could show me with her mind. I could even shift to unknown locations to find certain people with whom I shared a strong connection, but I couldn't take anyone with me for more than a few feet. If Patrick Mann got in too deep, I couldn't shift out with him. My choice might come down to leaving without him or dying with him.

"So," I tried to swallow past the clot of terror in my throat, "you're giving me backup, right?"

"Something like that." Ava pointed at Keene. "Mari, meet your brother."

Was she serious? Keene and I looked nothing alike. I was only one-eighth Japanese, but I'd kept Stella's family's slight olive coloring and the heart-shaped face. My long hair was dark, if not perfectly straight, and my eyes were decidedly brown. Keene was much lighter in coloring, from his hair to his green eyes and the skin that was a far different shade of white, even when he'd been out in the sun too much. He was tall, while I was a good foot shorter, and despite all the hours of grueling training, I didn't have anything approaching his lean muscle.

"Sure," I said. "Everyone will buy that."

Keene gave a slight snort. "If they're blind."

Ava nodded at Stella, and another holographic image flickered to life above the table. I peered at it, barely recognizing the woman with auburn hair and green eyes as myself. The man with matching auburn hair and trim beard threw me for a loop. Okay, so maybe it would work. With my high metabolism, I'd have to use a lot of hair dye.

If I lived long enough.

Something of my fear must have radiated in my face

because Keene leaned over and put his arm around me. "Hey, sis, let's do this thing. Piece of cake."

My stomach did that weird little flopping thing again, which had to be left over from my years as a mortal when I'd been shy and not accustomed to men taking notice of me. Except for Trevor.

"Okay," I said, "but can I have bacon on that cake?"

He groaned. "More bacon? Really? Okay, fine. Whatever you want."

"Chris is already prepping the plane," Ava said, ignoring our little exchange. "You'll leave for the airport at eight, sleep on the plane, and get there bright and early. I'm also sending Cort and Jace along for backup and to work with the New York cell. If there's any kind of emergency, the New York cell may be able to provide additional people, but they are already swamped with all the Hunter and Emporium movements there. I'd send more of our people, but everything is on edge here just like it is there, and we need to keep a strong presence on this side of the country or the Emporium will take advantage of our absence. Stella will, of course, be in regular contact with Patrick through the Internet."

"So, I guess I'll go pack," I said.

"About that." Ava's face relaxed into a smile. "Stella has some plans to help you get ready. Hope you're up for a visit to the salon and then some shopping."

Right. I'd need red hair, and I guess my usual attire wouldn't be up to presidential standards. *Great.*

Keene laughed at my expression. "Sorry."

"You too," Stella said. "I sent you an email about your appointment with a guy named Rogero. He'll set you up with your new look and supplement your wardrobe."

Keene groaned. "You gotta be kidding."

I couldn't help my smirk, thinking that he should be accustomed to such treatment. As the son of an Emporium Triad member, he'd been raised with the best of everything.

Everyone was up now and moving toward the door. I stood more slowly, waiting until Stella rounded the table. Physically, my great-aunt was only thirty-two, a year older than I was, but she'd celebrated more than two centuries of life, and I looked to her as a mentor. I needed her wisdom now. We walked down the hallway for a moment in silence, the others disappearing from sight. I itched to shift to my room on the third floor, or anywhere else but this tight hallway. Only worry held me back.

"So why isn't she sending Erin?" I asked finally. "If I stayed somewhere nearby, Erin could channel my ability, and she's a lot better at combat, especially when she channels Jace or Ritter." In fact, Erin's ability to channel others' gifts, essentially using them as her own, made her potentially the most powerful Unbounded to Change in a millennium.

"She was a possibility," Stella admitted, "but even though Patrick is no longer staying at the White House, the president wasn't keen on having a woman who can force her way into people's minds interacting so closely with his family and the politicians who are actually doing their jobs. Besides, Erin is far too well-known by the Emporium. She could channel Patrick's ability and alter her appearance using nanites, but maintaining that cover would be a huge distraction for her during a conflict. And then there's Ritter. Hiding him from both the Emporium and Hunters would be even more of a challenge, and Ava doubted he'd stay put here without Erin. Not until he gets over the fact that he almost lost her. Besides, we need Erin and her ability in the political meetings here. There's too much disquiet."

Stella paused, giving me a gentle smile. "Mari, you're the right one for this job—no, the only one. We weighed every option, including using Unbounded from the New York cell. Their leader and Ava, along with the rest of us, all came to that conclusion."

A portion of the weight on my shoulders lifted. "Well, truthfully, it sounded kind of fun before Ava got all serious."

Stella laughed and put an arm around me. "That's *her* job—keeping our minds on the goal. I've been wishing I could go with you because you know how I worry, but I really think you'll enjoy the experience, and that's the best kind of op. With Keene there, you'll be in good company."

Truthfully, I thought it was rather strange that they'd send a mortal who could be killed, but Keene had gone with Erin on a major op in New York, so maybe he was that experienced. He'd absolutely best me any day in a fair fight, and probably in an unfair one as well. His inner knowledge of the Emporium and his former infiltration of the Hunters gave him added advantage.

Still, what if I messed up and he was hurt? Cort and Jace would be in DC, but maybe too far away to help.

Stella came to a stop. "Look, frankly, I wish we'd had more time to prepare the world to know about us, but we'll do what we have to, and that's making sure mortals see us as allies and not as a danger."

Most of the Renegades felt the way she did, that the announcement had come too soon, but I was glad the secret of our existence was out to the mortal world. I wanted to be accepted for what I was, not what I'd been. A mere four months had passed since my Change, but already the life I'd lived as an accountant seemed a faint memory, one I didn't care to hold onto. I didn't miss being cooped up in an office all day or trying to convince Trevor that it was time to move forward with our family, never realizing that he was a Hunter and wouldn't stoop to having a child with me.

All that mundane stuff was gone. The clients, the daily grind, Trevor's lies. Everything but the numbers. They were still with me, in me—and my life was so much better. I wanted to shout my joy to the world and use my ability whenever I felt like it, not hide in the shadows and hope no one noticed I was different.

"So about the shopping," I said.

Stella looked at me for a full two seconds before she replied. For Stella, that was an eternity. "Oh, a few hours ago, I sent instructions to the salon and the boutique, so they know what you need. If anything, I've erred on the side of too much. I'd go with you if I didn't have monitoring to do, but Ava promised to see if Erin would go. I'll drive you to the airport later, though."

"All right." Was it just me or was she distracted? Stella processed information so quickly that normally she came across as being three steps ahead of everyone no matter what else she was doing or thinking at the time. But several times of late, I'd caught her delaying like she had just now. I'd wondered if that was because of Chris Radkey, our pilot and Erin's older mortal brother. Stella had been spending a lot of time with him and his two young children. Well, I could only hope he was the reason. She'd lost too much in the past months, and I wanted her to be happy.

Stella hugged me and brushed a light kiss on my cheek before moving toward the stairs, probably heading to her suite on the third floor. Her neural headset blinked furiously, signaling that she was already back to work.

I reached out to find Erin, first making sure that the numbers for the shift didn't match up with the location of her bedroom. Or Ritter's separate suite. Since their marriage two months ago, I was far more careful about where I located her because they were almost always together.

Erin was one of the few Renegades I could find no matter where she was. I could also shift to Dimitri, and more recently to Cort and Stella. The more I worked with someone, the more vibrant their location in my mind. They were actual numbers themselves, but unlike regular locations, their numbers represented colors, similar to hex color codes. Erin was a shade of vibrant red, Dimitri a steady brown, Cort a medium shade of blue. Stella had been orange, but now she was both orange and yellow, though I didn't know a reason for the change. The other Renegades I couldn't "see" yet, but Cort was sure it was only a matter of time as I worked more with them.

Erin was downstairs in our expansive workout room. I chose numbers that made sure I'd come out near the wall. Before solidifying completely, I always checked to see if I was shifting to a place already occupied by a person or object and could alter my location at the last moment. It didn't hurt anyone for me to almost appear inside them, but it was unsettling for both me and the person. I still didn't know what it'd do if I solidified inside someone, and it wasn't a phenomenon I planned on investigating any time soon. Appearing close to the wall generally assured free space. It also kept me clear of whoever might be attacking Erin, which was a common occurrence.

Sure enough, Erin and Ritter were at it again, exchanging blows with their escrima sticks at an incredible speed that told me she was channeling his combat ability. They were beauty in motion, each twirling two sticks, blocking and slamming in an odd dance that also radiated sexual tension. Their faces, necks, and bare arms glistened with sweat. Ritter's black hair was completely soaked, while the top portion of Erin's long blond hair, swinging free, was still partially dry.

The instant I appeared, they altered their positions slightly, their momentary glances measuring me as if I were some dangerous foe, but there wasn't a noticeable change in their ferocious play. Both continued moving for nearly a minute after I appeared, and then, as if by some silent agreement, they stopped simultaneously, chests heaving under their workout tanks.

I was glad they were on my side.

"Hey, Mari." Erin lowered her sticks. The color of her hair, the shape of her face, and even her eyes looked like Ava's. Funny how the same gray eyes seemed so much warmer on her.

Ritter dipped his head in greeting. "What's up? Want to have a go?" He spoke as if offering me a great favor.

I wasn't the only one on edge from the past two months of relative inactivity. Ritter was our ops leader, and like all combat Unbounded took downtime poorly. He had increased our four a.m. workouts from two to four hours, and if Erin hadn't kept him occupied with other endeavors, he probably would have doubled that yet again.

"No, thanks," I said. "But you should know that I'm now engaged to Patrick Mann."

Erin laughed. "Oh, so that's why Ava's asking me to go shopping or somewhere with you." She made a face, which I understood all too well. She didn't enjoy shopping like most women.

Her silent communication with Ava, wherever our leader was at that moment, reminded me to pull my shield over my thoughts. At first, shielding had been awkward, like trying to close my ears until I heard a rushing sound in my head, and had required a lot of effort. Now I barely noticed when my block was in place. Living in the same house as two sensing Unbounded, especially one as strong as Erin, we all blocked as a matter of course. Only when shifting did I have to drop the shield or it would interfere with the numbers.

"Sorry," I said, "but I could really use the company."

"It'll be good to go somewhere besides those boring political meetings." She laughed. "But seriously— engaged? I never knew you had it so bad for Patrick."

"Me and thousands of other women apparently."

She whistled. "Wow, Ava just showed me. Now that's scary." She gave her escrima sticks to Ritter, who was grinning, so I knew she'd shared the image from Ava with him.

"Take Jace to the shops with you," he said. "He needs to release a bit of energy."

I gaped at him. "You think shopping's going to do that? He's worse than Erin." Jace definitely shared his sister's lack of shopping skills.

Erin laughed. "No, but he can patrol the streets. And it's better that he work some of his energy out before you get on the plane. It's a long flight to DC."

"With all that's going on out there," Ritter added, "it's better to go in a group. The Emporium has figured out that we've rebuilt this house, and it's only a matter of time until they come knocking."

Erin grinned. "I'd like to see them try to get in."

The Emporium had attacked our safe houses before, with fatal consequences, but the Fortress could withstand anything they could do without attracting too much attention—and a lot more. We were finished running.

"I'm just going to jump in the shower," Erin said.

"Okay, I'll go tell Jace." I shifted away as Ritter kissed Erin goodbye. I didn't have to be a sensing Unbounded to feel the attraction pouring off them more copiously than their sweat.

I couldn't locate Jace yet by shifting, to his great annoyance, but sometimes I thought I could almost feel his color. Maybe a purple. Instead, I shifted to the second floor outside Cort's office, more from habit and a need to give Erin privacy than because I was trying to find Cort. I wasn't surprised at my choice. Cort and I had worked a lot together these past months as we tested the limits of my ability. His talent was to see and understand how things interacted on a quantum level, but he hadn't been able to figure out why I couldn't take anyone with me when I shifted.

At first he'd hypothesized that because I couldn't shift more than I could comfortably carry, I also wouldn't be able to shift distances longer than I could physically walk within a certain period of time. But that wasn't true— I'd shifted from locations several hundred miles away without straining a muscle. I just reached for the numbers that represented where I wanted to go and moved myself to that place using the *in between*. It felt like a blink or an involuntary breath. Simple.

So in theory, I should be able to move someone with me, and not being able to do so felt a lot like failure. But even when Erin channeled my ability and we shifted together, we could drag someone with us only as far as the next room—less distance than we could physically carry that same person. I'd tried repeatedly to choose different numbers to take us farther away, but we'd always ended up dropping randomly out of the shift.

I pulled out my cell phone to call Jace. The Fortress was big and he could be anywhere on its three floors or in the basement, which had a playroom and a climbing wall for Chris's kids. I should have looked there before leaving the basement, but Jace could just as likely be outside, either alone or in the gardens with his niece and nephew. We had a hundred-year-old tree that was the largest I'd ever seen anywhere, and the kids loved to climb it.

I'd punched in Jace's number and brought the phone to my ear when Keene's raised voice reverberated from Cort's office. "I can't do that!" he said. "I won't! Not until it makes a difference."

"I think you're making a huge mistake. It could mean life or death."

"Yeah, *her* life or death. I don't want to risk her."

Cort's snort was loud enough to hear through the door. "That's funny coming from you, Mr. Honesty. She should have something to say about it. This could give us a huge advantage in the battle ahead. We all have to make sacrifices. Maybe your inability doesn't have anything to do with why you don't want to tell her. Have you ever thought of that?"

"You have no idea what you're talking about!" Their voices were louder, so they were either near the door or the heat of their argument was increasing.

"You *have* to tell her," Cort said, his voice lower now but firm.

Keene's response was so low that I didn't hear.

Her. Who was this "her?" I couldn't imagine Keene being able to hide anything from Ava and Erin for long, and Stella was Ava's closest confidant. So who could it be?

Me? My stomach dropped.

"Hello? Hello?" said a voice in my ear. "Mari, can you hear me?"

"Where are you?" I asked Jace.

"In the garden."

The office door knob began to turn. I shifted.

CHAPTER 3

JACE WAS OUT IN THE MID-APRIL SUNSHINE. THE TOP OF HIS white blond hair reflected the light, while the lower half lay dark and wet along the edges of his face and the back of his neck. He held a sword in one hand, so I knew he'd been practicing. Despite all our guns and advanced tech, often with the Emporium it came down to swordplay and who was faster. Jace was our youngest Unbounded Renegade, having Changed at twenty-eight, and was talented in combat. His quickness rivaled Ritter's.

When he spied me, he pulled the phone away from his ear, pocketing it in his black sweatpants. "What's up?"

My mind churned, trying to figure out what I'd heard, what Keene was hiding. I couldn't imagine that it was anything regarding the Emporium, but he had served them nearly his entire life, and Cort had sounded worried about the battle. I felt sick not knowing. And sicker that I'd shifted away before demanding to be told. That was more like the old, mortal me. Not me after my Change.

Jace sheathed his sword and put his arms around me. "Mari, did something happen? You're so pale." He held me closer than I felt comfortable with, especially given how much he always flirted. Unlike the gray eyes of his siblings, Chris and Erin, Jace's were blue, with faint white patterns that made him seem perpetually alert.

I returned Jace's hug and forced a smile. "Just came to tell you that I'm engaged."

"What?" With an exaggerated gesture, he put a fatalistic hand to his heart.

"Yep. To none other than the president's son."

"Patrick?"

"That's right." He listened as I gave a rundown of the op. "I'm sure Ritter will brief us in more detail on the plane tonight. He's with Ava now." I stepped back from his tightened grasp. "First—and please try to contain your thrill—I have to go clothes shopping, and apparently you're coming along."

He laughed. "Good, I could use a package of socks. No time to do laundry."

"Sorry, we're not going to Costco." Jace was a huge fan of one-stop shopping, and the retailer was where he bought everything except his weapons. Anything to save time that he could then spend on training, ops, or bugging me.

"Well, let's get it over with then." Jace gave me a wink.

"It's warm enough that afterward we can stop for ice cream."

BY THE TIME WE FINISHED A VISIT TO THE HAIR SALON FOR my new auburn look, and took care of my wardrobe, spending more money in a single day than I'd spent on clothes in all of my thirty-one years, I was more than ready for ice cream. Following Jace's directions, Erin drove us to a new place called *Unbounded Café*, which boasted one hundred and fifty flavors.

"I drove by this place last month when they first opened," Jace said. "I've been wanting to check it out ever since."

"Guess they needed the Unbounded angle to open an ice cream shop in the winter," Erin said dryly, arching a brow at the six employees. They dressed in dark clothing, wore long leather coats, despite the warm day, and carried realistic swords in sheaths on their backs.

"Like some kind of cult," I whispered, fighting a sensation of unease. "Anyway, we don't look like that, do we?" Jace was dressed in a dark button-down shirt, but his slacks were lighter gray and he wasn't wearing a coat. Erin was actually wearing a flowing green dress, while I wore a slim navy blue dress I'd borrowed from Stella. Not a sword in sight.

"Well, we do dress that way on ops," Jace said. "They must have copied it from the Emporium agents the government recovered in Morocco. At least they don't have assault rifles." He sounded almost disappointed.

The café was full of people even on a late Wednesday afternoon, and some of the patrons also dressed in dark clothing, though, unlike the employees, I couldn't see any swords among them.

"Well on this next op," I told Jace, "I'm wearing five hundred dollar suits and dresses. And only one is black."

"Five hundred was the cheapest," Erin reminded me. "Good thing we got the jeans for only two."

Jace let out a disgusted sigh. "Only? Man, you know how many pairs I could have bought at Costco for that?"

The employees and patrons followed our progress into the shop to the back of the short line. Being Unbounded not only meant we had the very best genes our lineage could offer, but we also radiated the confidence and vitality that came with the Change. Mortals translated this into beauty. At first, the constant gazes gravitating my way had been unnerving, but now they only amused me.

"No Unbounded here." Erin's sensing gift allowed her to recognize our kind instantly. Knowing none were present, I found myself relaxing before realizing that being in the shop had made me tense.

The staff was surprisingly fast, and we arrived at the front of the line in less than five minutes. I ordered Endless Strawberry, Jace had Boundless Blueberry, and Erin had Unbounded Preferred Pistachio. Other flavors included Cherry Change, Triple Combat Chocolate, Regenerative

Raspberry, Immortal Mudpie, and Absorbed Apple, which I thought was rather gross. Unbounded could absorb the nutrients they needed to exist from the air and other substances, but I wouldn't want to eat anything someone else had already absorbed.

"No one ever asked me what kind of pistachio I prefer," Jace muttered. Erin bumped him with her shoulder as she handed a credit card to the brown-haired man behind the register.

With the receipt, the cashier gave her a flyer. Erin glanced at the paper before passing it to me. "A meeting to learn more about Unbounded?" she asked, her eyes ever-so-slightly losing focus, which I guessed meant she was looking at his thoughts.

"The end is coming," he said. "But the Unbounded can't be killed, you know. They can save all of us."

"I thought Hunters are claiming that cutting Unbounded apart kills them," Erin said.

The man snorted. "Hunters are liars. Sent to destroy our faith. You can't believe anything they say."

"I see." Erin turned away, her face blank. Jace tried not to snicker.

"Hope to see you at the meeting," the cashier called after us. "We'll explain everything."

When we were out of earshot, I waved the flyer. "They even have a prayer session."

"So, not a cult but a religion?" Jace asked, his mouth twitching.

Erin gave him a flat stare. "You'd like that, wouldn't you?"

I sighed. "Well, the guy's right about the end coming. It'll be the end of everything we know if the Emporium have their way." We'd been heading to an empty table, but I suddenly wanted to be far away from here. The idea of people praying to us was utterly insane. "Look, let's get out of here. We can eat this on the way back to the Fortress."

"Okay," Jace said, taking a bite of ice cream, "but I have to say, this stuff is really good."

We changed direction at the same time a commotion began at the shop's entrance. Five burly men dressed in jeans and long-sleeved flannel shirts had come inside and spread out, blocking the door. Two wore cowboy hats and boots, while the other three sported baseball caps and tennis shoes. The shirts and the hats bore the Hunter insignia of a man with a rifle.

Jace signaled me to cover the group on one side, while he took the other. Erin stayed in the middle. We were still some distance away, and the line of people were between us and the Hunters. Jace sized up our competition, the grin on his face predatory.

Talk first, Jace. Erin's warning came into my mind. I hadn't dropped my shield but despite my efforts, Erin could still break through. She had assured me that my shield would withstand an Emporium mental attack, but her ultimate goal was for me to keep her out, even in an emergency such as this. I dropped the shield completely now, sure that Jace already had. His combat instincts would have reminded him that Erin was our only way of silent communication.

No weapons had been drawn, but that didn't mean they weren't carrying. I was almost sure they were, and probably big guns with more rounds than permitted by restrictive California gun laws. Concealed weapons permits were obtainable in rural areas, and lawful everywhere, but most people in the city didn't carry. Fortunately, today, the bad guys weren't the only ones carrying. Not that we'd need guns to settle this. I much preferred the knife I'd already released from the sheath under the long sleeve of my borrowed dress.

"What's going on?" The brown-haired cashier came from behind the counter. "If you want to be served, please get in line. No reason to block the door."

"Oh yeah? We'll block it if we want, monster-lover," said the largest of the Hunters, who stood a foot taller than his companions and the cashier. He was one of those wearing a cowboy hat, but it was new like his boots, and I bet for him it was a costume purchased only because he'd joined the Hunters.

"Please." The cashier twisted his hands together, swallowing noisily. "We don't want trouble. I'm going to have to ask you to leave. Just like I did your Hunter friends who visited us last week."

The man and his friends chuckled. "Well, you can *ask* all you want," mocked the second man wearing a cowboy hat. He had a twang in his voice that said his worn hat and dull boots might be the real thing. The other Hunters nodded vigorously, joining in on the laughter.

"You see," said New Hat, "we come to teach you a lesson. We're from the same stock as those Unbounded monsters you worship. They tortured our fathers for not having that devil gene. We know the truth about their plans, and for the past sixty years we've been huntin' them. Before any of you even knew they existed, we kept you safe. They ain't gods. They're devils. And if you don't have the good sense to understand that, we're going to beat it into you."

The weapons came out.

New Hat had a knife in his large hand, but the other four men pulled out guns, each covering a separate direction. A murmur of fear rippled through the two dozen or so people in the shop. With two steps, New Hat grabbed the cashier and placed him in a headlock, knife to his cheek.

"Nobody move," twanged Worn Hat. "We ain't gonna hurt you. Leastwise not too much." Again his companions seemed to think that was the best joke they'd ever heard.

One of the others reached over and pulled the sword from the cashier's back sheath. "It's not even real. It's metal, but not sharp. Not like the real ones Unbounded use to cut people up." No twangy accent or poor English. This was probably some local college kid.

Erin's gaze fixed on the big Hunter, and he suddenly barked, "Put away your cell phones. Now. Everyone.

Don't even think about taking pictures or calling the police."

"Do what he says!" yelled College Boy, waving his gun.

Little too late for this precaution, since several minutes had already passed, and I suspected this was Erin's way of making sure whatever we did next wasn't recorded. She could suggest thoughts and release them inside people's heads, and sometimes it worked.

"So, you worship Unbounded, huh?" New Hat taunted the cashier. "Where are they now? You think they're going to come down in a beam of light and save your sorry ass?"

"They'll rid the earth of scum like you!" retorted the cashier.

I had to hand it to him. He had a lot of courage, and even if his faith didn't make sense to me, he was right about our ultimate goals.

"I thought you might say that." New Hat shifted and pressed his knife into the cashier's belly. The man's screams were accompanied by those of several patrons. Wetness appeared on the cashier's black shirt.

I plopped my ice cream on a table and stepped around the woman in front of me, who took the opportunity to flee to the back of the shop. More patrons followed, pressing themselves against the wall. I didn't see any cell phones among the terrified faces. I stopped moving about five feet from the two Hunters on the left wearing baseball hats. The young men held their guns nervously, and I hoped they didn't shoot someone on accident. Or on purpose.

"You can't be a real Unbounded," New Hat told the cashier. "I've never seen one squeal like a stuck pig, even when we cut them apart. They scream and curse, yes, but no squealing."

Worn Hat pulled a small chain saw from a bag over his shoulder. "Folks, you have nothing to fear. We're just going to show you how to get rid of an Unbounded devil. Don't worry. It doesn't really hurt. They don't feel like we do, though, as my friend said, he may holler a bit. Ladies, you might want to cover your ears." He took a small video camera from the bag and tossed it to College Boy.

A sinking feeling entered my gut. These men had come here to make a statement. They didn't care that the cashier was only pretending to be Unbounded. They were going to hurt him. Apparently they were willing to go to jail for their cause.

Erin eased closer to me. *Mari, the big guy's yours. I'll take the two on the left. Jace has the two on the right. When I begin the distraction, shift.*

I let the point of my knife slide further into my palm, the metal feeling cool and inviting in the crowded shop. Anticipation rolled through me.

Erin took another step and reached her hands toward the chain saw. "Oh, let me! I want a chance at the monster. All I did was buy ice cream and he tried to seduce me into his cult. Wants me to bear his Unbounded child!" She waved her hands energetically as she spoke, her green dress fluttering around her, showing a lot of leg. The patrons gawked in fascination at the violence in her face and voice, while the Hunters checked out her legs.

With her distraction, I shifted, reappearing behind the big Hunter, the door to the ice cream shop at my back. He laughed suddenly, finding Erin's behavior amusing. Maybe he was even contemplating taking her up on the offer. I stepped close, one arm wrapping around him, slipping the knife up under his right ribs. The metal gobbled at his flesh and beckoned for more. *Not today.*

He gasped, struggling for breath. Which only caused more pain and more struggling. He was lucky. A few more inches and I could have hit something more vital, but Hunters were mortal, after all, and despite my hatred of them, killing this man wasn't going to solve our problems with his group or with the Emporium. Besides, my fellow Renegades kept reminding me that Hunters were part of the humanity we were trying to save.

"He's having a heart attack!" I screamed, replacing my knife in my sheath and pushing him down to the floor.

Erin and Jace were already taking the guns from the remaining Hunters. Erin moved as fast as Jace, so I knew she was channeling his ability. Jace couldn't resist a few punches that sent his Hunters sprawling, their eyes rolling up in their heads. Erin produced a couple of long plastic twist ties to restrain hers.

Abandoning the Hunter, I knelt next to the fallen cashier, lifting his black T-shirt to peek at his wound. It was bleeding but not deep. "You'll be okay," I told him.

He pulled me down to whisper in my ear. "You're one of them, aren't you?"

So not going to answer that one. "Do you have a surveillance camera?"

"Yes."

"Erin," I began.

She was already kneeling next to me. "Where does the camera feed to? Is there a password?"

"The office," said the cashier. "I can't tell you the password . . . unless . . . Please, are you—?"

"Shh." Erin placed a hand against his lips as a picture of the office appeared in my thoughts. *Password is Unbounded. Meet us in the car afterward.*

I jumped to my feet and began pushing my way through the crowd that had converged as patrons and employees craned their necks to see what was happening. As soon as I was past them and sure no one was paying attention to me, I shifted to the location Erin had shown me.

My last glimpse was of Jace using the phone behind the counter.

CHAPTER 4

PART OF OUR RENEGADE TRAINING WAS IN ELECTRONICS because we often had to cover our footsteps when Stella wasn't around. On the office computer, I easily found the file connected to the camera in the ice cream shop. I stopped the feed, selected the file, and connected to an online corruption virus Stella had created. In minutes, it was finished.

Sirens were already wailing in the distance, which meant it was time to go. With a tissue from the desk, I wiped down the computer keys I'd touched, just in case. Then, taking a piece of chocolate from a dish, I popped it into my mouth, chose the coordinates of Erin's Jeep, and shifted.

Erin and Jace were there, but Erin was on the phone. "It's Ritter," Jace informed me. "He knew something was up."

I wasn't surprised. Ritter and Erin had developed

a connection that sometimes happened to sensing Unbounded and their mates. The connection intensified when there was trouble to one or the other of them.

"I bet she just loves that," I said, slipping into the back seat next to one of the outfits I'd purchased, still covered in plastic. We'd sent the rest ahead to the plane packed in tissue and boxes, but this one I planned to change into before we landed in DC.

Jace snorted. "She likes it like a hole in the head." He passed me an ice cream cone. "I got a few more before we left."

"That's good. I left mine on a table back there."

"By the way, nice knife work on that Hunter."

"Collapsed lung," I said. "Could be life-threatening."

"Doubt it. Unfortunately, they got to him in plenty of time."

Erin hung up and put the Jeep into gear. "Ritter says they have the streets around the shop blocked. Apparently we weren't subtle enough getting out of there. Either that, or they're worried about more Hunters. But we should be clear here. We're parked far enough away."

We drove without incident to a warehouse several blocks from the Fortress. This was our back door. The man who had originally built the mansion had been a public works manager when San Diego was in its infancy, and his business expertise was only equaled by his paranoia. He'd built tunnels under the wide expanse of lawn, reinforcing them with concrete against high water levels, and connected them to both the sewers and his newly built mansion—intersections he'd conveniently left out of the official plans. The tunnels also connected to this warehouse, and it was especially useful in masking the odd hours we sometimes kept.

We'd reinforced the original tunnel setup with metal doors, handprint readers, security cameras, and explosive charges that could be activated in an emergency. The front entrance of the house was even more heavily guarded with remote machine guns in the trees and inside several decorative statues, more weapons on the roof, and explosives in the yard. We also had a newly created electronic security field that prevented sensing Unbounded from seeing inside and shifters like myself from passing through. I felt safe there, the way I'd once felt with Trevor.

I wanted to be there now, not traversing the secret tunnels, but I wouldn't be able to get past the shields, so I stayed until we entered the basement. Then I shifted, leaving Erin and Jace to debate the benefits and drawbacks of an Unbounded religion. They'd know immediately that I'd gone, but everyone accepted my impatience for traveling in the conventional way.

There was really nothing left for me to do before the flight but to change out of Stella's dress, check the material for blood stains before returning it, and gather the few things I'd need from my room, namely my collection of knives and sheaths. They'd probably make me take a gun or two as well, much as I hated the things, and I wondered how we planned to get any of it past

Secret Service, who had shadowed Patrick Mann since his return from Europe.

Instead of in my room, I appeared once again outside Cort's office. Okay, so that was not what I'd been planning. Or maybe I had. Apparently, I needed to discuss what I'd overheard earlier, as much as I wished I could forget it. There were no voices inside now, and I tapped at the door.

Until Cort called, "Come in," I hadn't realized that I'd been hoping he was away so I could search his office for clues. Blowing out a frustrated sigh, I pushed into the room.

"Hey, the red hair looks great. All done shopping?" Cort eyed the plastic-covered outfit I carried on its hanger. He gave no indication that he'd heard of the excitement at the ice cream shop, and I wasn't about to enlighten him.

I tossed the rest of my ice cream into an industrial-sized trash can near where he had several experiments set up on a wide counter. "Look, about Keene," I said. "Is it just me, or does he seem different these days?" Since Venezuela, I meant.

Cort regarded me calmly for a few long seconds before he responded. "Do you have something specific you're referring to?" None of the emotion I'd heard earlier when he was arguing with his brother came through in his voice or expression, but after living five hundred years, maybe you learned a little about poker faces.

"Not really." I certainly wasn't going to tell Cort

about being squeezed into that closet with Keene. Before that day in Venezuela I'd been thinking about Cort as a possible future partner, but that was when I'd realized it must be the old me who found Cort attractive because he'd never made my blood rush in my veins like it had that day in the closet with Keene. Which was just as well, because I'd begun to suspect that Cort found me a little flighty.

"Hey, since you're here," Cort said into the silence, "I've been thinking that maybe we should test your ability in the vacuum of space." He thumbed toward the ceiling. "Maybe up there you could move more than just yourself."

Leave it to the logical Cort to narrow in on the flaw to my talent on the day before my big op. "Yeah, I guess. Let me know when you send off the next space mission."

Cort didn't catch the sarcasm. "Sure."

For all I knew, he had the connections to arrange it. "Excuse me. I have to finish packing."

"Wait." Cort's hand shot to my arm. "Look, Mari, something *is* going on with Keene. Just keep an eye on him. Sorry, that's all I can say."

The information was woefully inadequate, and we both knew it. I wondered if Keene had been using the drugs Cort and Dimitri had experimented with in an attempt to activate the Unbounded gene in descendants who hadn't Changed. Could something have gone wrong? Cort was clearly not going to answer me, so I wouldn't ask.

"Right." Still holding Cort's gaze, I shifted.

My room appeared around me, and I started gathering my belongings. This morning I'd purchased just about everything I'd possibly need, but I was definitely taking my feather pillow. I'd had that thing since fifth grade, and I didn't sleep as well without it. The end of several feathers poked out of the material, which told me it was time for a new cover.

I was all ready to leave when a soft tap came on my door. "Come in," I called from the couch. My TV was on, though the sound was off, and the wannabe mothers stalking Patrick Mann filled the screen. I dropped my left hand where I'd been gnawing at the soft flesh of my middle finger between the beginning of the palm and my middle knuckle.

I expected Erin or Stella, but instead it was Keene, an easy smile filling his lean face. His brown hair had been cut and dyed a realistic auburn, and they'd done wonders with makeup because the scruff of slightly darker auburn beard looked longer than it had earlier. Unlike Unbounded who often shaved two or three times a day, he wouldn't have been able to grow it that fast, unless Cort had provided him with some advanced hair serum I didn't know about.

"Wow," I said, coming to my feet. "I almost don't recognize you." They'd also done something with the scar that had run vertically on the side of his face near his hairline, because for once the hair wasn't covering it, but the scar was nowhere to be seen.

"I could say the same thing about you." Keene whistled. "You look great! I mean, you always look great, but red really makes you look different."

"They even did my eyebrows. The green contacts will be waiting for us in DC, though."

"That'll be interesting."

For the first time, I noticed the dinner plate in his hands, covered by a silver food dome. "Come have a seat," I said, going to my sofa. "What's up anyway?" The words Cort had said about Keene being different came rushing back. Maybe Keene was here to confess whatever he'd been talking about with Cort. Maybe I *was* the "her" they'd referenced.

He sat next to me, setting the dinner plate on my lap. His hands brushed my thighs, seeming to burn through the material of my jeans. My eyes snapped to his, locking into place. The green enveloped me and sent more parts of my body into flames.

Exactly the same thing had happened in that dark closet in Venezuela.

I swallowed hard, pushing my thoughts back. Away. Anywhere. I hadn't felt this aroused since first meeting Trevor, who had betrayed me in the most horrible way. Now it was Keene who had secrets.

Tell me, I thought.

He swallowed hard. "Hey, sis—I'd better get used to calling you that, I guess—I brought you something."

So, no confession. Maybe there was nothing to confess.

But there had to be. Life or death, Cort had said.

He might be distracted with his experiments, but Cort had never been prone to exaggeration.

Keene held my eyes. My heart thundered in my ears. The whirling emotion made my fingers itch to touch him, to have his arms around me like in Venezuela. *Not going to happen,* I thought.

"Well?" he asked, his voice taking on a touch of uncustomary nervousness. "Aren't you going to see what's inside?" He looked pleased with himself and unsure at the same time.

I tore my eyes from his and stared down at the dome. Whatever was inside wasn't horribly heavy but definitely solid enough to put pressure on my legs. Securing the plate with one hand, I used the other to grasp the knob on the dome, lifting it.

Inside was not one piece but an entire small cake. Chocolate frosting layered the sides, but on the top, the frosting was waved in the shape of bacon, red and white frosting marbled in with the chocolate.

"Your cake with bacon, Madame," he said with a little dip of his head. His eyes were now dancing.

I swiped a taste of the frosting. Sure enough, my nose hadn't fooled me—the flavoring was bacon, and not an extract but probably from the fat of real bacon.

My anger at him fled as I laughed and hugged him awkwardly around the cake. "How did you manage this?"

"I'll never tell." With a flourish, he produced two forks.

I took a bite of cake as he looked at me, his brows drawn. "Well?"

"It's delicious." I took another large forkful and some of it didn't quite make it into my mouth. Keene reached over and wiped his finger over my bottom lip, rescuing a mound of frosting.

He put it into his mouth. "Mmm. It is good."

I tried to agree, but my voice stuck in my throat. I couldn't take my eyes off him, and his didn't leave mine. *What did Cort mean by a matter of life or death?* I should just ask Keene, but whatever had stolen my voice wouldn't let me.

"To our upcoming op," Keene said, lifting another forkful of cake. "I think it's going to be fun, even though we're going to babysit a spoiled rich boy." His voice was confident, and his smile wide, but there was something in his eyes I couldn't read. Longing? Fear? Or maybe just that stupid secret.

"What, you mean rich boys like you?" I taunted.

His smile vanished. "I guess you could say I had everything but the right genes." A hint of mockery filled his voice, not directed toward me but at himself. I knew how much it had hurt him all those years to have not Changed, to realize that even in the Emporium where his father had so much power, he was a second-class citizen. That wasn't why he'd deserted them, of course, but doing so hadn't healed the raw hurt of being rejected by your own blood. I wondered if he ever regretted defecting to the Renegades to work with his brother. I knew they both had mixed feelings about their father.

I scooped up a piece of cake and put it in his mouth. He did the same for me. Every nerve in my body stood at attention. His eyes drank me in every bit as much as if he were touching me. At that moment I wanted nothing more, secret or no secret.

"Mari," he said, his voice hoarse.

"What?" My voice was as rough as his.

"You have chocolate on your shirt."

"Thanks." Standing, I went to the closet for a new T-shirt, glancing back at Keene, whose eyes followed my every step. I changed in my closet and returned. He was standing now, staring at the TV screen.

"Jace says you guys learned about a new Unbounded religion today." His fist clenched and unclenched at his side.

"Looks like it."

He sighed, his eyes finally meeting mine. "Does it bother you working with a mortal?"

"No." It was only a partial lie. It bothered me that he might die because I wasn't good enough, and it bothered me that I was worried about trusting him—except trust didn't really have anything to do with him being a mortal.

He crossed the steps between us, energy spilling from every stride. His hands went to my upper arms, slightly chafing my triceps. "Mari, I . . ."

I waited, but he shook his head once as though flinging away a thought.

Maybe Keene was still hung up on Erin, despite her recent marriage. I knew they'd been close before she and Ritter had become serious. Or it was entirely possible Keene had met someone new. Maybe this new woman was the one he'd been talking about with Cort. Could she be a danger to our Renegades?

His hands dropped, leaving me cold. "I'd better get downstairs," he said. "I promised to help Ritter with the extra weapons we're bringing along. We may need them during the op, and it's almost time to leave."

"Eleven minutes." I left off the twenty-four seconds because no one appreciated a show-off. But Ritter would already have the equipment ready by now, and we both knew it was an excuse.

He smiled. "Remind me never to pick you up late."

I returned his smile and watched him go without asking the question burning on my tongue. Whatever Keene was hiding, I was going to find out. I'd protect Patrick Mann, even if it turned out I was protecting him from Keene.

CHAPTER 5

STELLA DROVE US TO THE PLANE IN OUR ARMORED VAN, STILL wearing her neural headset. At the airport before I could get out of the van, her hand fell on my shoulder where I sat in the passenger seat. "Hey, can I talk to you for a minute?"

The others were already grabbing their gear and heading for the hangar. Keene glanced back at me and then at the empty tarmac around us, as if double-checking for Emporium spies or other dangers. At the hangar door, Jace said something to Keene and remained there, waiting for me.

"Look," Stella began, "I know this op may take more than a month or two. There's no telling when I'll see you again."

"I'll call every day." Looking at her now reminded me of the woman I'd known as a child, who pretended to be my mother's friend but was in actuality a relative. It was because of her that my mother had received Unbounded sperm when she'd decided to go to a sperm bank to have a child. I was grateful beyond words, but after my Change, the shock of seeing her again, as young as ever, had been no small thing.

Stella laughed. "You guys still treat me with kid gloves. I'm okay, you know."

"I know." But I didn't really. She'd been devastated at losing her unborn baby to an Emporium raid, and days later her mortal husband to a rare immune disease. Occasionally, I'd felt smothered by her interest, but she was my ancestor, and I wanted to help her through it.

"I'm pregnant," she said.

I blinked. "What?"

"I decided it was time."

"So your husband left frozen—"

"The baby is Chris's."

"Erin and Jace's brother? That Chris?" Since Chris was flying us to DC, that might explain why she was so eager to drive me to the airport.

"Yes. With sperm manipulation, we have a forty percent chance of our child carrying the active Unbounded gene. That's better than I had with Bronson. And my baby will need a good dad, regardless."

"Oh, Stella, I'm so happy for you!" I reached over and hugged her.

Before my Change, I'd been trying to talk Trevor into having a child, and the desire for a baby hadn't completely vanished after my Change. Now there would be a baby sooner than expected. Not mine, but almost as good. Like Chris's children, this new baby would belong, in part, to all of us.

"Does Erin know?" I asked. "What about everyone else?"

"Erin and Ava, of course." Stella laughed. "Can't hide a life force from them, and Dimitri helped in the lab. Ritter knows because of that last op in Morocco." She paused before adding, "I'm almost three months along. I just wanted you to know before I started looking like a whale."

I gave a snort. "Yeah, right."

"I'm glad you're happy for me. I was worried about telling you."

I frowned. "Because of Trevor."

"Yeah."

"Don't worry about that. I wouldn't change what I have now for a dozen lifetimes with that jerk. It's just as well he didn't want children."

She laughed again. "That's the spirit. Come on. I'll go in with you. I want to say goodbye to Chris."

Something in the way she said his name called my attention. When she'd talked about the baby, it seemed more of a business agreement with Chris, but if I added in the tone of her voice just now and the time she'd been spending with him and his kids, maybe there was more to it. Before my mind could come up with the question I wanted to ask, she was already out of the car.

I hurried after her, and Jace opened the door as we approached.

Inside the hangar, Keene and Cort were loading gear, while Chris had a panel of the plane open and was doing something with a screwdriver. When he saw us, he pocketed the tool, ran a hand through his dark blond hair, and came toward Stella, his eyes riveted on her face. How had I not noticed this?

I was fiercely glad Stella wasn't curling into a ball and giving up after losing her husband. She was going on, and by the smile on her face, I'd say that Chris was halfway to winning her, lab baby or no.

As the others loaded the plane, I remembered something I'd forgotten, so I made a quick stop in the hangar restroom. Shifting the moment I stepped inside, I chose numbers that would move me instantly to a place miles away. There, I appeared in my usual place near a display and the end of an aisle that hid me on three sides. If anyone was near, I could usually shift again before they could look my way. This time, I was behind a man who was intent on reading the details on a box. The soft pop alerted his attention, but I stepped forward to make it seem I had just rounded the aisle.

His head swivelled toward me, surprise registering on his round face. "Oh, I didn't see you. Am I in your way? You need one of these blenders? I hear they're good."

I shook my head. "No thank you. I'm looking for socks."

"Better hurry. In case you didn't hear, they already announced that they'll be closing soon."

"Thanks."

I was back in the hangar before anyone noticed I was gone. I handed the package of black socks to Jace.

"Wow, thanks! I thought I was going to have to borrow Cort's."

"They'd never go with your jeans."

"I know, right?" He grinned. "Is this where you were just now? Man, your ability is a thief's dream."

"Hey, I paid for those."

He laughed. "Does this mean you'll go out with me? I mean if you're getting me socks and all."

"You're too young."

"What's three years in two thousand?"

"Ask me in another century then." I think Jace had gotten into a kind of fantasy about asking me out. Maybe one of these days I should say yes because he was right about the age difference being moot, and he could always make me laugh. We were a lot alike.

"Ready?" Cort asked everyone as he stored the last bag. Nods all around, even Stella, who wasn't going with us.

To our surprise, Chris bent down and kissed Stella full on the mouth. We all pretended not to notice as we filed up the stairs and into the plane. Chris was the last one inside, and he waved to Stella as he hit the button that would pull the stairs inside the belly of the plane. She turned away as he began sealing the door.

This was our larger plane, the corporate jet, though it wasn't as large as many companies employed. It also wasn't as luxurious, but a far sight more comfortable than our smaller plane, and as the fiancée of the president's son, I had to arrive in some semblance of style. On the right of the aisle were two sets of four facing seats with a table between each of the four. On the left side there were only two facing seats separated by a smaller table. Ten seats in all. Behind the two chairs on the left we had a small kitchen and beyond that an even smaller bathroom. A storage area took up the rear of the plane, including tightly fitted metal bunks where we often transported Emporium prisoners who had been temporarily killed in battle or heavily sedated. I was glad we had no such prisoners today.

Hanging the outfit I carried in a special compartment near the door, I grabbed a place in the first set of four seats, pushing my bag underneath. I had a novel in the bag, but I didn't know if I'd be able to concentrate. Keene dropped to my side. For the moment, we were alone because Jace and Cort were in the cockpit with Chris, both determined to learn more about flying. Cort could fly our smaller plane well enough, but the larger plane for some reason made him uncomfortable, so he was practicing when he could. The plane felt empty without Erin, Stella, and the others. I sprang up to get myself a drink, sat down, and then went back again to the small kitchen for another glass for Keene. He nodded his thanks but didn't drink the water.

After what seemed like hours, but my ability told me had only been thirty minutes, we were up in the air. I felt anxious already, penned in. I wished I could just shift to DC, but I wasn't familiar with our destination, and I truthfully didn't know if it was possible to shift that far. I'd crossed cities, but not states, and certainly not the entire US. I hoped the worst that would happen, if I couldn't shift that far, was that I'd drop out of shift early like I had when trying to take someone with me, but even that meant there was no way I'd attempt it from the plane. I might survive a thousand-foot drop, but it would hurt every bit as much as it did for a mortal when I hit the ground. For now, I had no choice but to spend the next seven hours on this plane. I'd never been claustrophobic, and I wasn't now, but I hated that I didn't have options.

Cort and Jace returned to us, slipping into the seats opposite Keene and me. "So," Cort said, "who do you think is responsible for the attempt on Patrick's life?"

I was glad for the distraction. "Hunters," I said. "Or the Emporium, I guess."

Keene considered a moment, leaning partially over the table with his arms on his knees. "The Emporium certainly has the power, and my gut says they're behind it, but we must consider that having Patrick make nice with the American people is actually a plus for them."

"I have to agree," Jace said. "No matter how much the Emporium hates him, they'll want that good will, so I'm betting its Hunters. We've seen how much they hate us—all of us. They won't care about Patrick being the president's son or that he claims to be a good guy. They'll only see that he's Unbounded, nothing more."

I thought of the employees at the Unbounded Café. "Apparently, Hunters aren't just targeting Unbounded anymore. Not if what happened at that ice cream shop today is any indicator. The guy in charge as much as admitted he knew the employees weren't Unbounded."

"Well, they were pretending to be Unbounded," Jace said. "And they started a religion around us. That's got to spell danger to all Hunters."

"A lot of people have joined the Hunters since the announcement." Keene ran a finger around the top of the water glass I'd given him. "I'm not so sure their leaders are in complete control anymore. New Hunters could have been behind the shooting attempt on Patrick. Experienced Hunters and the Emporium would both know that a bullet couldn't kill him, and that with so many Secret Service around, they weren't going to have a chance with just one shooter to kidnap him."

We let that bounce around in our heads for a moment, and then Cort broke the silence. "So our best bet is newly joined Hunters. We need to look for a connection. But we still can't overlook the possibility that it might be someone we aren't familiar with."

"An unconnected third party out for private vengeance?" Keene's voice was doubtful. "Maybe a politician or a few together might have enough power, but they'd likely be backed by Hunters or the Emporium. And it's doubtful a person working alone would be able to get past Secret Service."

"I was thinking more along the lines of another group," Cort said. "Or maybe two groups. The girl found in Patrick's room at the White House might not have been a threat. Maybe she was a gift."

"You mean from someone who likes us?" I asked.

Jace scowled. "Unbounded worshipers. Ugh."

"What about the knife she was carrying?" I could feel the comforting weight of those strapped to my wrists beneath my long-sleeved blouse. They were made of tough plastic instead of my usual metal ones, because it turned out the Secret Service would be checking us for weapons in DC. Once at our destination, I'd retrieve our regular weapons from Cort, who I could shift to wherever he was staying. "People don't usually carry knives unless they're prepared to use them."

"Well, the knife was obviously why they thought she was there to hurt him," Cort said, "but she wouldn't have had to take her clothes off for that."

I shrugged. "Unless she thought seducing him was the only way to get close enough to use it."

"Cort's right that we need to keep an open mind," Keene said. "Missing some connection could mean his life. Patrick was a businessman before he was taken by the Emporium, so it's possible he already had enemies."

"Or that his doppelganger made enemies, more like,"

I said. "That guy was insane. He pretended to be Patrick for an entire year, so there could be dozens of businessmen who want to cut his throat."

"Right. Until we've eliminated all threats, you'll remain with him every minute." Cort tapped a briefcase on the table. "You'll use the machines in here to check his foods for poisons—without alerting the Secret Service to what you're doing. I've already shown Keene how to use these, and he'll show you once you get there, Mari. We can't have someone from the inside incapacitating any of you."

"Sounds good." I'd keep watch for everything, but I still thought Hunters were behind this mess with Patrick, and I'd be more than happy to ruin their plans. I stood up with my empty glass and pushed past Keene, his knees rubbing against the back of my legs. He didn't move to make it easier to pass. "Anyone want something to drink?"

Heads shook, but I continued my path to the kitchen and filled the glass with water. Leaning back against the sink, I chugged it down. At this rate, I was going to spend half the flight in the bathroom, which would only intensify my trapped feelings. I brought my left hand to my mouth and bit the soft skin on my middle finger. I didn't close my eyes for fear that I might see Trevor.

I'd become catatonic after finding him, and four months after Dimitri and Erin had brought me out of it, I still had nightmares. In them, Trevor and I'd be snuggling together watching television, or making dinner, and he'd look at me suddenly, his head falling back to expose the slit in his throat that sometimes opened and shut like a mouth. Occasionally, we'd be back in the park where in real life he'd handed me over to his fellow Hunters. In the dream, he watched them rape me, the gaping cut laughing and spurting blood. Erin didn't arrive in time to save me like she had in real life. In the most frightening dreams, I was the one slitting his throat with the knife, instead of the Emporium. Yielding to the blade's seductive power and enjoying every second. Becoming like the very monsters I fought.

I bit harder on my hand. More than anything I wanted to shift, to see the numbers. To be anywhere but trapped in this confined space.

"One of these days you're going to bite that clean off," Keene said, pulling my hand from my mouth and holding it between both of his. One finger rubbed against the slightly swollen part where I'd been chewing. His touch was gentle.

"Helps me think." The habit came from before my Change, something I'd given into when working on the most complicated business taxes, only then, a large callus had formed. Now my metabolism renewed the skin before much damage could occur. It was like being allowed my vices without the consequences. Eating as much bacon as I wanted and knowing that it would take more appetite than I could work up to ever gain weight.

Keene didn't let go of my hand, and I pulled gently away, fearing the pounding of my heart even more than I did the nightmares.

"I brought cards," he said. "Come on. Let's play."

"I don't feel like it."

"That's because you're afraid you'll lose."

Something in me rose to that. "You wish!"

"It's either cards or you can just pace back and forth and make everyone else as anxious as you are."

"I'm not anxious!"

"You always are. Every time we fly. Or drive long distances. Or when we're on lockdown in the Fortress."

I hated that he knew me so well.

"Come on," he urged. "Let's go for it."

I knew he meant the cards, but I felt myself flush. "All right then."

I stalked back to the table to find that Jace had moved to the other set of four seats and was watching something on the table's retractable screen. *Probably a Rambo or Terminator movie,* I thought. Cort was laying out Keene's cards.

We played for hours, far more than either Keene or Cort wanted to play, I could tell. I was the tally keeper, of course, and they both asked me repeatedly to add the long columns to see who was winning, which only took a glance and a few seconds. Cort was always in the lead. I felt annoyed at their constant attention, but the games and the adding did take my thoughts away from shifting out of there. Finally, my eyes grew tired, and I laid my head against the wall next to the window. The next thing I knew, I was drifting off.

I awoke sometime later to a firm touch on my shoulder.

"We're almost ready to land," Keene said. He was seated opposite from where I lay; I was now extended over the two seats on my side of the table, a space almost wide enough to be comfortable. Cort and Jace were nowhere to be seen—probably in the cockpit with Chris.

Keene had changed into dress pants, a button-down shirt, and a light jacket, all casual clothing with muted tan colors but great lines. "Is that new?" I asked him. Was it me, or had the hair on his face grown since takeoff?

He grimaced. "Most of what I brought was left over from my Emporium days, but this tan stuff—yes, definitely new. The rest isn't this color. Thankfully." He smiled. "You slept well."

I'd been too tired even for the nightmares, for which I was grateful. I pushed myself to a seated position. "Guess I'd better change."

"Yeah, apparently there'll be a press conference at the airport after we land."

"This early? It's not even six a.m. on the East Coast."

"Nope. But Patrick will be there and that's news." He hesitated, and I suspected there was more, so I waited. "Look, this was all sort of sudden, and I don't know that Patrick is prepared, or that his fiancée is willing to lend her ring, so Cort and I thought . . ." He stuck a hand in the pocket of his light jacket and pulled out a ring box. "It's been in our family a few years, and it's real, so don't toss it when this is over."

I blinked at the engagement ring. "That's at least two carats."

"Three." He chuckled. "Totally believable for the society we're about to enter. Should go well with all the other costumes."

I laughed with him because the clothes and the ring did feel like costumes. Trevor and I had bought our wedding bands for two hundred and fourteen dollars on sale. For both of them.

I slid on the ring, which was slightly large, but the band was thick and I didn't think it would be a problem. "Okay, I'll be careful with it."

"Better hurry. You know how Chris likes to stress seatbelts upon landing."

I retrieved my makeup kit, shoes, and my outfit and made my way to the bathroom, which I needed quite urgently after my long nap. I'd forgotten about my new hair, and I almost didn't recognize the woman in the mirror. The salon had done a great job, and the makeup certainly accentuated the difference. With my hair swinging free and the confidence in my step, I looked the part of Patrick's fiancée.

Still, uncertainty crawled across my shoulders. I had only one chance to get this right. Patrick's life—and maybe Keene's—depended on me.

Showtime, I thought. With the entire world watching.

CHAPTER 6

THIRTY MINUTES LATER I WAS POKING MY EYES WITH semi-permeable contact lenses that somehow made my brown eyes a dark green. I'd worn contacts before as part of our training, so I knew the routine, but placing them took longer than expected. Finally, I dabbed away the tears, reapplied makeup, and was ready to go.

Cort handed Keene my bag. "Patrick has the wireless earbuds that will connect you two to him at all times while you are out on visits. Before that, of course, you'll need to get your regular weapons from me."

Jace gave me a hug and whispered in my ear, "One swipe at the emergency button and we'll be there for backup. We're staying on the same street."

Unless they were out helping the New York Renegades, but I wasn't going to say that aloud. I could tell by Jace's actions that he was feeling uneasy about the op, that he wished he was the one pretending to be my brother. He was a demon at fighting, if a little rash, so I understood the sentiment. But Keene was more experienced with Hunters and the intrigue that surrounded the Emporium.

"We'll be fine," I said, hugging him back.

Jace glanced over his shoulder to where Cort and Keene were heading toward the door that Chris was preparing to open. We'd picked up our contact courier in another location and had taxied to where the media and Patrick Mann awaited. Like Keene and me, Chris was in disguise in case anyone snapped his picture. Cort and Jace would stay on the plane with Chris until the press was gone or more likely until the plane was secured in the hangar loaned to us by the New York Renegades.

"Mari," Jace said turning back to me, his voice almost inaudible. "Keep an eye on Keene, okay?"

I stiffened. "What do you mean?"

"It's just, well, he's still having a hard time about those people in Morocco who died because of the explosion."

"That wasn't his fault."

He hesitated a tad too long. "No, but he seems to think it is."

"Okay." My thoughts tumbled against one another. Obviously, Jace believed Keene had something to do with the explosion in Morocco, but I didn't see how that was possible.

Was I the only one who didn't know what was going on? The answer seemed just out of my reach, like a puzzle

I had all the pieces to but simply wasn't connecting. I'd have to think on it a bit more.

The door to the plane opened, bringing a whiff of exhaust fumes and jet fuel. The sun hadn't yet risen, but gray morning light leaked over the horizon. Two Secret Service agents insisted on coming inside the plane. They didn't frisk us, but they did run a metal detector over our bodies and the bags we were taking with us now. The plastic knives in my thigh sheath and my two arm sheaths went undetected, but they had to thoroughly investigate our food-testing equipment. After the agents were satisfied, Keene ducked through the door and turned to offer me his arm.

Here we go. I hurried forward, the spiked heels of my pumps biting into the carpet. I emerged at the top of the stairs and cameras began flashing. I smiled and waved.

Patrick Mann rushed up the stairs, meeting me halfway with an exuberant hug. He was different from the Patrick Mann I'd met in New York last December. That man had been wounded and bruised, the devastation in his eyes emphasized by the pallor that came from a year of imprisonment. Being able to absorb meant that he hadn't starved, but the physical abuse had been horrendous. Now, the devastation had been replaced with eagerness, and the paleness with a healthy glow.

My hug was real and so was his. "So good to see you," he whispered. "Thanks for doing this."

"My pleasure," I said. He was tall enough that I had to look up into the blue eyes. Dark brown hair framed a pleasant face whose best feature was a generous mouth that tended toward smiles.

He leaned down to kiss me, to the clapping of the crowd. A quick, chaste kiss that gave me a whiff of cologne and only the briefest pressure on my lips. Then he was shaking hands with Keene, whose eyes scanned the crowd and the tarmac behind them. He paused more than once on each of the additional half dozen Secret Service agents waiting below.

Looking for threats. I briefly touched one of the knives under the sleeve of my off-white suit, appreciating the security they gave me.

Taking my hand, Patrick Mann led me down the stairs, and when we reached the tarmac, he addressed the reporters. "I guess you're all wondering why I had you come out to the airport this morning." He paused and gave a little laugh. "Well, mostly it's because I don't want any of you showing up at my house." Polite laughter rippled through the group.

"Where are you staying now anyway?" someone shouted from the crowd. "We heard you left the White House."

Patrick grinned. "I'll never tell." He paused a moment before going on. "But I want to confirm rumors that I am engaged to the very beautiful Marianne Pendross. I'm not going to go on about her charity work or the accounting firm she works for—I'm sure you can find out about that yourselves." Again the little laugh. "I just wanted you to know why I plan to spend every minute I can with this beautiful woman."

Questions from the crowd, one louder than all the others. "I see you've already picked out a ring."

Without faltering Patrick lifted my hand. "We have indeed."

"When's the date?" called another reporter.

"Well, I wanted tomorrow, but Marianne has some idea of getting a dress"—Patrick spread his hands out helplessly—"and flowers and maybe a little food. I don't know. Ask us again in a month or two."

"Is she Unbounded like you?" asked a woman in front. "How does she feel about marrying someone who really isn't human?"

"Ah!" Patrick held his hands to his heart as if he'd been wounded. "I assure you, I'm every bit as human as you are. 'If you prick us, do we not bleed? If you tickle us, do we not laugh?'" The crowd cheered at the Shakespeare quote, and I could understand why Patrick was chosen to be the face of the Unbounded. He played to the crowd all too well.

Fortunately, no one seemed to know the rest of the quote: "If you poison us, do we not die? And if you wrong us, shall we not revenge?" Poison would do no long-term damage to any Unbounded, and the idea of Unbounded revenge was terrifying.

Then again, poison would stop an Unbounded temporarily until something more drastic could be done, which was why we carried equipment to test for it, and mortal revenge could be every bit as ugly. We really weren't so different after all.

"As for whether or not my being Unbounded bothers my fiancée," Patrick continued, "well, I'll let her speak to that."

The microphones shifted slightly in my direction. I tossed my hair over my shoulder with a careless flick of my head. "Think of it this way—I get a man who in my lifetime will never get sick, grow old, or lose interest. What do you say about that, ladies?" A little cheer went up among the women. More seriously, I added, "I think our lives and our relationship will only be that much more fascinating with the Unbounded dimension." Now I paused to make sure everyone was listening. "But I'll say one thing to all of the women out there—I'm the only one having his babies! So back off. You'll have to find your own man, Unbounded or otherwise. Patrick is taken."

A murmur of approval ran through the crowd, almost drowned by the sound of clapping. I laughed, not even feeling the need to shift away. The wide sky had completely alleviated the trapped feeling I'd experienced on the plane.

"Who's the man with you?" asked another reporter.

"This is my brother, Kenton. He's my chaperone." I winked at the cameras as they all laughed. "At least until the wedding."

Patrick raised his hands, and the attention shifted back to him. "Thanks, everyone. If you'll excuse us now." He put his arm around me and rushed me to a waiting limousine, flanked by Secret Service. Keene hurried after us.

"That was perfect." Patrick handed me into the car. "Really perfect."

"Had me convinced." Keene's eyes dropped to our linked hands, and then away, as he slid into the seat facing me. Patrick climbed in next to me and we were off.

Patrick's grin didn't go away. "It really is great to see you guys. Lucinda about had a heart attack when everyone said we needed to go public."

"And she's really okay with this?" I didn't see how she could be.

Patrick laughed. "Yeah. I think so—unless you suddenly develop the hots for me."

"I think I might be able to contain myself," I said dryly. "If I try really hard."

"Just let me know if you can't."

Keene rolled his eyes at the exchange, but I was already having fun.

"Truthfully, I only told Luce last night about the added protection," Patrick said. "She seemed okay with it. Guess you'll see for yourself. She's waiting at the house."

If she wasn't okay with the situation, it'd make my job all that much harder. "Keene and I—Kenton and I—will do our best to make this easy on her."

Patrick flashed me a grin. "That's reassuring. And I'm glad it's you. Could have been awkward, but I think we'll do just fine."

I glanced at the soundproof glass separating us from the two Secret Service agents riding in the front. "We were told they don't know why we're really here."

Patrick rolled his eyes. "Oh, no. They'd take that as an insult. They honestly believe you're my fiancée. Still, you don't know what it took for me to make sure they didn't pat you down for weapons. They are quite dedicated to their jobs. I had to keep reminding them that we were getting married, that you could smother me with a pillow or something, if you wanted to. By the way, they know Luce and I are friends, but I've mostly kept her away from them since we got back from Europe and they were assigned to me. If they ever suspected something else, that will change now." Patrick shifted enough to pull out his wallet. "Since yesterday, I've been helping Stella plant information on the Internet about you and Luce being friends and us meeting through her. I'm actually hoping this situation will give Luce and me more time together." No mistaking the heart in his eyes as he handed me a photo from his wallet.

Lucinda Ririe, Patrick's real fiancée, had short blonde hair, striking cheekbones, pale blue eyes, and a rather large nose. She was beautiful in a classic sense, definitely model worthy, despite the lack of makeup. In the photograph, she was looking off into the distance, as if embarrassed to be a bother to whoever was taking the picture.

"She's beautiful," I said, passing Keene the photograph.

"I think so. You'll meet her when we get to my house—or rather the place where I'm installed at the moment. I thought it best to get away from the White House, after what happened with that girl. The press hasn't found me yet, but it's only a matter of time until they do. Everyone seems to have eyes in DC. I have four Secret Service with me at every minute, and another two who come on outings." For the first time, I caught a glimpse of something besides the cheerfulness he'd displayed. Patrick Mann was doing what he had to do for the world, but he wasn't happy about it, or at least not all of it.

Keene handed back the photograph and pulled out his phone to briefly check his texts. "My contacts verify that there isn't any official Hunter hit out on you, but that doesn't mean some of their new members aren't going off on their own. So, until we determine where the attacks are coming from, we'll need you to make a list of any business dealings that might have put you on someone's hit list."

Patrick's face took on a slight green cast. "That guy who took my place when I was held captive made serious enemies. More than one or two. I tried to make it right with everyone when I got back in control, but some people aren't easily appeased. And some things you can't give back." He sounded both sick and angry, and I knew there was more to the story, maybe something personal, but I wouldn't press now.

Keene obviously agreed. "Get me the list, and send

Stella a copy. I know you're a technopath, but she's been dealing in information a lot longer than any of us."

Patrick didn't show any annoyance at the curtness in Keene's voice. "Tell me about it. Stella makes me feel like I'm back in kindergarten."

"That, we can all understand." Keene's eyes fixed on something outside the window. "Looks like more fun up ahead. Maybe we'll get to knock some heads together after all."

"You sound like Jace," I retorted. His comment made me uneasy. What was I missing? I looked out the window where we were passing a security gate to see another crowd waiting on the other side—people who hadn't been allowed onto the airfield with the press. Curiosity seekers and women with suggestive signs. Worse was the knot of rough-looking men with the telling Hunter symbols on their hats and clothing.

Time to start earning my pay. I reached for my purse before I remembered that my nine mil was back in a hidden compartment on the plane with the rest of our normal weapons. Instead, I pressed the release on one of my arm sheaths, allowing the knife to slide into my hand. The weight was different from my regular blades, but the enhanced plastic would cut through flesh and meat just as well.

Patrick put his arm around me, pulling me close, trying to look relaxed. "In case those women can see through the glass," he explained. "The sooner they quit lusting after my genes, the better."

We all tensed as the car pressed slowly through the crowd, the bumper nearly touching several sign-holders. One man shoved his crazed face against the darkened glass of the window next to me, screaming obscenities, but we got through without further incident. Rather a letdown with the adrenaline zipping through my veins and the energy filling the limo. I could see numbers in my head without trying, and I had the crazy notion that I could shift the entire car to any destination of my choice.

"Sorry, I thought it would be better having you fly into Dulles instead of National," Patrick said. "But it looks like more people besides the reporters got wind of my pending announcement."

"Should calm down now that we're almost through," Keene said.

But things weren't calming down, at least not for me. Numbers filled my head, the car, the faces of my comrades. A sound must have come from my throat because Patrick's arm tightened around me and Keene leaned forward, his face creased with concern. "What's wrong?"

I didn't know what was wrong. Most of what I knew about my gift I'd discovered through trial and failure. I'd never met the only other Renegade shifter, who'd died in Europe of old age shortly after the president's announcement. By that time, he could barely shift across a room. As far as I knew, the Emporium had no shifters. Mine was one of the rare abilities that both Renegades and the

Emporium had been trying for decades to revive. There was no one I could ask or learn from. For all I knew, this could be some fatal side effect of using the ability.

I could see Keene's number color was green. Green as in rebirth, green like growing, green meaning balance and a tendency toward martyrdom. I could *see* Keene. I could see him more clearly than anyone. Not only him, but the others in the car, though the green was the clearest.

What the hell was going on?

Then, all at once, I knew. It wasn't me . . . it was Keene. The others had hinted, but I hadn't understood. Keene wasn't just acting different, he *was* different. He had Changed. Beyond all hope or expectation, he was Unbounded, and all this energy was coming from him. The fact that I hadn't realized what everyone else knew made me furious at myself.

And at him.

Keene removed his seatbelt and put his hands on my shoulders. "Mari," he shouted, "what is it?"

"Stop," I told him, unable to catch a breath. "Too much."

Whatever he was doing was strangling me.

CHAPTER 7

THE NEXT INSTANT, THE PRESSURE WAS GONE, ALONG WITH the numbers and the colors. My lungs filled with blessed air. I stared into Keene's eyes, the emerald color dark in the gray interior of the limo. A flitting anger passed over his face. He released me abruptly and sat back.

"You okay?" Patrick asked, running a hand from my shoulder to my elbow and back again.

"Yes. Sorry." I breathed deeply. "Sometimes I get a little claustrophobic and my instinct is to shift."

Keene's nostrils flared, and I knew he was affronted with the lie. Keene didn't lie, except in my book with-holding the truth was every bit a lie as telling a whopper.

I held Keene's eyes as I added, still addressing Patrick, "I was seeing numbers like I never have before. Couldn't you feel the pressure?" Keene and I were *so* going to have this out when we arrived at wherever we were going.

"To be honest, I did feel something," Patrick's voice was subdued, respectful. "Even the agents up there were looking back."

Let him think it was me, all that power. What gift did Keene have to affect me and Patrick that way? It both scared and exhilarated me. It had to be what Keene had been arguing about with Cort.

I knew his color now, his coordinates, and it only took the barest effort to find the number that would shift me next to him. Like it did with Erin and Dimitri. I couldn't find Patrick or the agents, though, perhaps because I hadn't focused on them when it was happening. But Keene could probably help me find them.

Suddenly, I laughed inside, careful not to show it on my face. When I was finished being angry at him, we would do a little experimentation. First, I needed more information—but not with Patrick staring at me like he was just the slightest bit afraid.

Forty-five minutes and much traffic later, even at this early hour, we arrived at his place on S Street. Meaning twenty-seven thousand square feet of house on three quarters of an acre. In Washington DC the cost of the place would be astronomical. But not only was Patrick a businessman in his own right, he also had the backing of all the Renegade cells and the US president.

The house itself was rather ugly, boxlike, and covered with red brick. However, what little I glimpsed of the gardens, before the car was buried in a detached garage, was enchanting. Inside the spacious entryway of the house, a checkered black and white rock floor met us with unremitting boldness. The round chandelier, bench, and numerous side tables filled with fresh flowers looked like something from a museum.

Several of the Secret Service agents hurried in front of us across the checkerboard floor to a set of double interior doors on the far side of the entryway, apparently checking for danger. The doors opened onto a wide hallway, where a multicolored rug ran down the middle of the floor, marring the bold of the black and white rock that continued through the space. More museum furniture, light sconces on the walls, large mirrors, and tapestries screamed wealth. Multiple doors connected to the hallway, and stairs led up to other areas of the house.

"Sorry," Patrick murmured, staring at a gilt-framed picture of some early political figure. "A little pretentious, I know. We bought it furnished. Come on, I'll show you to your rooms." He smiled at me as we started up the stairs after the agents. "You're in the suite next to me, of course, with Luce—hope you're okay sharing the suite with her. Your brother, uh, Kenton, is across the hall." He glanced at the Secret Service agent ahead of us to see if he'd noticed the hesitation, but the large black man didn't appear to be listening.

We had a slight delay as the agents swept the house, and the tension was high until we were finally allowed to enter my sitting room. Lucinda Ririe was there waiting for us, wearing a white dress with large blue polka dots and a matching blue sweater. As the door closed, shutting out the agents, she jumped up from a stiff Victorian love seat and threw herself at Patrick. "Oh, sweetie, I was so nervous. I saw you on TV, though, and you were wonderful!" Stars gleamed in her eyes as she indicated a muted TV nestled inside a dark entertainment center.

He kissed her with much more energy than he'd put into our kiss, and she kissed him back with equal passion. She was nearly as tall as Patrick and large boned. They made a handsome couple. "Luce," Patrick said, reluctantly drawing away, "I want you to meet Marianne and Kenton."

She leaned forward with a slight blush on her cheekbones and shook my hand. "Thank you so much for coming." Her voice was soft and cultured. "When Patrick told me last night they were sending someone, I was so grateful. I just don't do crowds well." She towered a head taller than me, but her grip was weak and boneless. Feminine. Everything in me that was Unbounded wanted to tell her to stiffen up a bit. Weakness meant danger.

"I knew it was a good idea, Patrick having a fiancée," Lucinda continued. "I mean, that girl somehow got past all the security at the White House. I'm glad his father and those over Homeland Security aren't leaving it only up to the Secret Service anymore. It's good to have another layer of protection."

Homeland Security? I waited for Patrick to correct her. The Secret Service agents were actually under the Department of Homeland Security, and they had other employees and associates who weren't Secret Service, but we weren't here with their knowledge. And although President Mann had been involved in the decision, he wasn't exactly calling the shots, either. He knew the Renegades considered Patrick family and would protect him without any kind of order.

I glanced at Patrick, who had opened his mouth, but he closed it again without speaking.

"It's nice to meet you," I said to Lucinda.

Keene shook her hand next and then removed an instrument from his bag and began walking around the room, testing for listening devices. He had been avoiding my gaze since the events in the car, and I let him for now. Still, I couldn't help watching him as he worked, his lean muscles taut and panther-like. For no reason at all, I thought of the closet in Venezuela. Had he already Changed then?

"Let's get some pictures for the media," Patrick said, motioning Luce toward me. She laughed lightly, and Patrick responded by kissing her cheek.

"Apparently, we're going to be best friends." Lucinda slipped an arm around me. "I know we won't have time for shopping and such, but I'm excited to tag along in the background to be near Patrick. I'm still hoping things will die down, though."

"They will," Patrick said. "Soon Unbounded will be just like any other race—even if that means I have to personally talk to every reporter and visit every school in the United States. Speaking of schools, I believe I'm supposed to speak at a grade school today."

"Oh, I hoped to spend a little time with you first."
Lucinda grimaced and even that looked queenly on her.
She may not like the limelight, but the public would love
her. Maybe I could help her move in that direction, so
after my future "breakup" with Patrick, she could face a
life in the limelight. If she loved Patrick, and I believed
she did, she'd learn.

Patrick took her hand. "We have until ten. That's
better than before, right?" He looked at me. "You don't
mind if I hang out here, do you?"

"Of course not. Enjoy yourselves. We'll just work
around you."

KEENE AND I CHECKED PATRICK'S SUITE, KEENE'S QUARTERS, AND
my own, finding no bugs. That was good news. Then we
had a large breakfast served in my suite, despite the fact
that no one had requested food. The cook brought it
herself on a trolley with elegant dishes that looked more
like they belonged in a museum than on our table. The
woman herself looked nothing like I thought a cook
should look. She was young and pretty with brown eyes,
her skin was faintly bronzed by the sun, and her willowy
figure looked more like it belonged to a dancer than a
cook. She appeared too serious, though, to even listen to
dance music.

"This is Susan," Patrick said, sitting beside me on the
couch. "She's been with me since Europe."

Susan dipped her head. "Nice to meet you. I hope you like bacon."

"Love it. Nice to meet you too." I reached for a piece of bacon before remembering that I wasn't back at the Fortress, but Susan simply handed me a plate and didn't comment on my lack of table manners. Keene pointedly took out the case Cort had given us on the plane to check for poisoning. Stifling a sigh, I put the bacon on the plate and reached for a napkin.

"Thank you, Susan," Lucinda said. "It looks so lovely, as usual."

"It's good to see you again, Miss Lucinda. Who would have known that you would introduce Patrick to his fiancée?" Susan gave a dry chuckle, her seriousness finally giving way to a smile. "But if that's what it took to bring you back to the States, then I'm doubly happy for him."

Patrick took my hand and stared lovingly at me. "Life is pretty amazing sometimes." He held my hand until the cook left, then stood and reached for Lucinda. "I'm glad we thought to tell her that you and Mari are friends."

Lucinda leaned toward him, offering her face for a quick kiss. "I already ate, so I'm going to my room to wash my hair and change for the school visit. I overslept this morning."

He squeezed her hand. "Hurry back."

Keene was already at work on the food, and Patrick watched with amusement as we used both food-testing methods Cort had given us—one an electrode of sorts that tested the entire surface, and one that mixed small samples with a chemical. The food was clean.

"Like I said, Susan's been with me for a long time," Patrick said. "She's had plenty of time to poison me, if she'd wanted."

"She's probably not the only one with access to the food." Keene busied himself putting away the equipment.

"She does have an assistant now, an agent provided by the Secret Service, and she's responsible for every bit of food brought into this house." Patrick forked up a bit of egg. "Almost seems easier for me not to eat." He was right, since we didn't need to eat to survive, but not eating would raise more red flags.

"Then I wouldn't get bacon," I said, taking a healthy bite. Keene grinned at my enjoyment, and for a moment things were okay between us.

After breakfast, our luggage arrived from the plane, brought by two white-liveried men, one of whom shook shaggy black hair out of his eyes as the Secret Service frisked him. Jace was obviously enjoying his own disguise, and he joked with the agents, who surprised me by cracking smiles. Soon, Jace and Cort were joined by a beautiful, very dark black woman with long, tightly curled black hair pulled into a ponytail. Her ugly uniform couldn't hide a figure that would be noticed anywhere, being so close to the world's ideal of the perfect female form: tall, long legs, overly slender torso except for the ample bustline, and a splendid, perfectly-shaped rear that made all of the Secret Servicemen look more than twice.

I recognized her at once, but waited until she carried one of the thoroughly searched suitcases upstairs to my suite before I hugged her. "Noah! I didn't know you'd be here!"

She laughed. "I'm the one who set up the house for Cort and Jace. I came with them to see you."

"I'm glad you did." I hadn't seen Noahthea Westmoreland since our last op in New York, three months ago. Unlike most Unbounded, her gift wasn't viewed as useful in the battle with the Emporium, but I secretly envied it. Noah had the most beautiful voice and for over a hundred and fifty years had regaled music lovers all over the world under several different identities. When she sang words, her audience felt them. When she mourned aloud, they cried. Her joy brought people to new heights. Listening to her sing was an experience I never forgot. I wished we weren't fighting the Emporium so that we could cultivate more talents like Noah's that lifted people, instead of trying to breed combat Unbounded destined to kill and maim.

"I was so glad when you and Keene accepted this op," Noah said. "I'd considered asking for the job"—she shook her head—"but you know how useless I am at protection."

"Yeah, but you would have had those reporters eating from your hand once they heard you sing."

She laughed and even that was musical. "Thank you for saying so."

Patrick had risen from the sofa to greet Noah as

well, and now he hugged her. "You have to say hello to Luce before you leave. She should be out soon. She just went to get ready for an appointment we have later this morning."

"Okay, I'll wait." Noah thumbed at Cort and Jace, who were bringing up a second load of boxes. "We'll leave the heavy lifting to them."

Patrick laughed. "Good idea. Thanks for the backup, guys."

"No problem." Jace placed a box in his arms. "Here, make yourself useful."

"Oh, that reminds me." Noah pulled a flash drive from her pocket and handed it to Patrick. "I made you a copy of the music I was working on while we were all in Europe. It also has all the variations that won't make it to the CD."

Patrick's face lit up even more. He set the box down on a table and grabbed the flash drive. "Oh, wow, thank you! I can't wait to hear the whole thing."

I began moving my boxes and cases into the bedroom part of my suite. Patrick and Noah helped as they talked, and it became apparent that they knew each other well. I was glad someone from the New York cell had remained in contact with him while he'd been in hiding.

Lucinda emerged from the second room in my suite as Cort and Jace deposited the last load inside my sitting room. Her short hair was fluffy now and slightly curled, her makeup impeccable. She wore an elegant gray pant-suit over a yellow top with a high neckline.

"Oh, good!" Noah said, rushing to her. "I was afraid I wouldn't get to see you."

"What a wonderful surprise!" Lucinda's gaze caught on Noah's white service jumpsuit. "I don't know how you arranged to deliver their luggage, but I guess I shouldn't be surprised."

"I pulled a few strings." With typical Renegade caution, Noah didn't introduce Cort and Jace or expose their identities, and Lucinda overlooked them completely. The two women clung to each other's hands. This close to Lucinda, Noah didn't look tall at all, but rather petite next to Lucinda's taller, more sturdy figure. But Noah held herself with the confidence of the Unbounded, and it was she who overshadowed Lucinda instead of the other way around.

"DC suits you," Noah said. "You look fabulous. Or is that because you're with Patrick?"

"That's it, probably." Lucinda let go of Noah and intertwined her arms in Patrick's. He winked at her, and she lowered her gaze bashfully.

"Looks like you'll finally get to spend more time together. I'm happy for you." Noah glanced at Jace and Cort, hovering by the door. "Well, I'd better get going. Maybe when things calm down, we can get together for real."

"I'd like that. We'll walk you down."

"Better not," Noah said. "We don't want the Secret Service taking notice that we're acquainted, or they might put two and two together and suspect something's up with Patrick's new fiancée. Today, I'm only a stranger delivering her luggage."

"Oh, right."

Cort made a motion at me, something about a gun and two fingers. He wanted me to shift to his location in twenty minutes to get our weapons from him. I waved goodbye, and they left my suite, trailed by two Secret Service agents waiting in the hallway.

As Patrick had only a minimal staff at the moment, I was thankfully allowed to do my own unpacking. Lucinda tore herself away from Patrick long enough to help me, exclaiming over the clothes and eyeing the name brands. "I'm afraid I'm going to look like the poor cousin next to you," she said with a laugh that was genuine but reserved like the rest of her. "Patrick gave me a card to use, but I just can't seem to waste so much money when something for half the price looks just as good."

"If it looks just as good," I pointed out, "no one will notice."

"I hope you're right."

I unwrapped a pale blue suit with a back pleat from its multi-layers of tissue and hung it in the closet. "My normal fare is much more casual. I used to have another job where I wore suits like this one all day, but they weren't fitted, and I looked like I was wearing a bag."

"Well, the one you're wearing now is fabulous," she said, eyeing the off-white material.

"Thank you." I would have preferred red or purple. Anything but blah. Unfortunately, the woman who'd helped us at the boutique had seemed to paint everything with the same brush. If it hadn't been for the red hair, I might have revolted.

"So, Marianne, how long have you known your partner? Or worked with him, rather."

"Call me Mari." I knew they picked the name Marianne because it was similar to my own, but the entire thing sounded like far too much effort. Like walking instead of shifting.

"Okay, Mari. So how long?"

"Four months."

She nodded, a shy smile curving her lips. "He's cute."

I blinked at her. She was checking Keene out? Then it dawned on me that she meant he was cute for me. I laughed. I was definitely warming up to this woman who seemed more like a reclusive princess than anything else. "Yeah, I guess."

She laughed. "You know you have it bad for him, don't you?"

"Let's hope the media doesn't think so."

"They won't. It's just a look I saw between you two, earlier. So am I right?"

I'd thought so, but his secret might have destroyed that forever. "I really don't know."

She shrugged. "Give it time."

Thinking of Keene made my anger come rushing back. He'd hidden so much of himself these past months. I'd thought the feelings between us in Venezuela had been real, but maybe it had all been in my head. Regardless, we were in the same Renegade cell. We were friends. That he hadn't told me hurt more than I cared to admit.

I glanced through my bedroom to the sitting room where Patrick sat on an uncomfortable-looking wooden chair, bent over papers he'd spread out on a round table. A phone pressed to his ear, and he was saying something I couldn't quite hear. "We have half an hour before we leave for the school," I said to Lucinda. "I need to talk to my partner about security."

Lucinda's pale eyes widened. "Okay, I'll finish here for you." Her voice lowered as her gaze also strayed to Patrick. "But you should really think about letting him know how you feel."

Oh, yeah. I was going to let him know *exactly* how I felt.

Excusing myself, I marched through the suite, nodding at Patrick as I passed him, wishing I could simply shift. It would have made for a much better scene, appearing before Keene had his defenses up, but for now I would respect his privacy. A Secret Service agent was seated in a chair near the window in the hallway. He studiously averted his gaze as I crossed the hall and rapped on Keene's door.

CHAPTER 8

AT HIS INVITATION TO ENTER, I WALKED INTO KEENE'S SITTING room where the double doors to his bedroom stood wide open. Like me, he had boxes with tissue paper and several suitcases. I did shift now, appearing an arm's length away from him. "So," I said, hands pressed on my hips.

He removed a shirt and shook it out, laying it on the bed before grabbing another. "What?"

"Why didn't you tell me?"

His eyes shut and opened slowly, sending unwanted heat coiling through my belly. "Tell you what?"

I yanked the shirt from his hand. "You *Changed*."

"You say that like an accusation."

"Does everyone know? Am I the last to find out?"

His jaw worked. "Yes."

"Why? This is good news, isn't it? Or do you really hate us?"

"No. I wanted to be Unbounded. All my life." There was a curl to his lip that hinted of self-loathing. "I wanted it too much. When I hit thirty-six, I realized it wasn't going to happen. I've never personally known anyone who Changed that late. The worst of it was the disappointment in my father's eyes." His voice sounded empty, as if all his hope had been consumed by that man I'd never met but detested. A little of my own anger died in that moment.

"But you did Change! How?"

He shrugged. "I'd been doing gene therapy with Cort and Dimitri, but if it was that, it only worked because of my direct heritage and all the sperm manipulation surrounding my birth. More likely, I'm just a late bloomer." His mouth turned slightly upward at the corners but his tone was mocking.

"Your ability. That was you in the car."

He scrubbed a hand over his beard. How could I have ever thought they'd done something to make it longer? If I looked closely, I could already see that the part closest to his skin was brown, not auburn.

"It's called synergy," he said. "I can see patterns in everything like my brother, but I don't understand how they work. Rather I see how to change them, mostly increase them." He grimaced. "Sort of like an atomic reaction."

The skin on my arms pebbled. "The explosion in Morocco. I thought that was Erin."

"It was both of us together. Her channeling Cort so we could see how to do it without taking down the whole building."

Why didn't you tell me? That was what I really wanted to ask, what hurt the most. Keene prided himself on being honest, and I knew he'd never voice an outright lie, but this felt like the biggest lie of all.

"In the car I saw your color," I said, pushing back the hurt to a place where it didn't make me useless and unwanted. "And I can still find you when I reach for a shift. That means it stayed with me, taught me something."

His expression hardened. "If you remember, you also couldn't breathe. Now quit mutilating my shirt." He pulled it from me.

"I didn't understand what was going on, that's all." I took a step toward him. "I forgot that I don't need my lungs to breathe, that absorbing works for oxygen too. I was never in any real danger of suffocating. If you help me using your ability, I might be able to find anyone. Maybe I could travel longer distances. Maybe I could take someone with me!"

"Maybe I could blow you up." He turned away, but not before I saw the firm set of his jaw. "You might end up in the middle of the ocean. Or on Mars."

"What are you talking about?"

He whirled on me. "I can't control it! It's unpredictable. I might just as well help the other side. It was my synergy that made that fire in Venezuela burn out of control, trapping us in that closet. And if Erin hadn't shielded us in Morocco, I would have killed us all!" Grief blazed from his eyes. "People died, Mari."

"You've killed before."

He nodded once, sharply. "The difference is that this time some of those who died were people I was trying to protect. People who were just walking by the hotel."

I understood what he was saying. In fact, I understood a lot of what I hadn't before. "But I'm guessing your ability is why they sent you with me. Ava wants us to experiment together. That's what you and Cort were arguing about." I *was* the woman they'd been discussing.

"You heard that?"

"Some of it." I clenched and unclenched my fists, trying to release my frustration. I hoped they had a gym in this mausoleum or I was going to go crazy if I couldn't shift whenever I wanted. "Look, whatever your reservations about your ability, this is *good* news. You're Unbounded!" I wanted to make him see—feel—what I did. From the moment I'd recovered from the trauma of Trevor's violent death and began testing my ability, the new me had just wanted to *live*. Everything seemed brighter, had more potential. I still couldn't wait to discover the entire world! Even two thousand years might not be enough time for all I wanted to do. Keene's fear only wasted time.

"Unbounded," he said with a little sneer. "It makes a difference to you after all."

My mind tried to catch up with what he was saying, tried to untangle his words from my hurt. "What do you mean?"

"This." In one step he closed the space between us, his hands clamping down on my forearms and pulling me against the length of his body. His mouth angled over mine, pressing downward. One hand slid around to the back of my head, pushing my face closer. The other cupped my back.

Energy crackled around us. Desire sparked all the female parts of me, urging my arms around his chest. I saw numbers, larger than even I could count. I experienced more colors than I had believed existed. I pushed closer, kissing him back, long and hard. Exactly the way I'd wanted to ever since Venezuela.

Venezuela.

I saw the combinations of numbers that would take me to that burned building where we would be alone, to finish this kiss where it should have begun. Or maybe we'd somehow stay in the *in between* for as long as it took to get our fill. I almost believed I could take him with me. The anger and hurt had vanished. I felt like laughing and singing and melting into him.

"Mari," he groaned against my mouth. Panic layered the word.

"Let it go." Only half aware of what I was doing, I pulled numbers toward me. The Venezuelan ones beckoning the loudest. The thrill of the unknown surged throughout my entire body, the rush of adrenaline every bit as intoxicating as his touch. I felt powerful. Filled. *Keene's synergy,* I thought. Emotions waved higher and higher to an impossible crest. The breathlessness was there again like it had been in the limo, but now there was a subtle difference. Keene was doing something different that didn't steal my breath completely. *See?* I wanted to say. *You can learn to control it.*

The kiss ended almost as abruptly as it had started. "What the hell?" Keene stared at air where another scene shimmered before us. Jungle, warm sun. Venezuela. His nostrils flared as he stepped away, arms dropping. The scene vanished, as did the kaleidoscope of colors and the numbers in my mind. The letdown made my knees sag before I stiffened them with the resolve that had gotten me through three years of marriage to Trevor.

"If I were still mortal, that never would have happened." Keene's voice was satisfactorily jagged, but his words once again made no sense.

"What? Why not? I've been wanting to do that ever since Venezuela. Wait, is this about you and Erin?" I was back to clenching my fists again, my body and mind screaming with anger. "Look, I'm not Erin. Maybe she chose Ritter over you because he's Unbounded and she thought you weren't, but I think it's more because they belong together. I think she chose him because for her there was no other choice, not with him alive. But I'm *not* Erin. I'll never *be* Erin. Maybe that's the real problem— that you can't get over her." I waved a hand as if I didn't care, hoping it wasn't shaking like my insides or my traitorous knees. "Whatever, but don't expect me to act like her. I think being Unbounded is the most incredible gift you've ever been given, but it doesn't change how I feel about you."

He stared, his eyes not leaving mine, mouth slightly ajar. *Wind out of his sails,* I thought. *That's right. Who's the woman now?* His expression was slightly lost, and I had the urge to reach out, to recapture the moment of the kiss. But no way was I ever throwing myself at another man, especially one who was obviously hung up on a woman who happened to be one of my best friends.

I'd rather fight Hunters with my bare hands and no backup.

"And for the record, you didn't almost kill me in Venezuela or Morocco. I could have shifted out at any time." I grinned—okay, maybe it was more of a smirk. "Guess now the next move is up to you. But not right this minute, because it's almost time to leave and I still have to get our weapons from Cort. Plus, I'm seriously annoyed at you."

I shifted to the door and yanked it open because I needed to be away from him. But as I stepped out into the hallway, glass shattered and an explosion rocked the mansion.

CHAPTER 9

I LANDED ON MY STOMACH IN THE HALLWAY. A PICTURE careened down the wall and slammed on the floor, barely missing my head. The Secret Serviceman was likewise on the floor, but stirring, so he wasn't dead. No time for the questions flooding my brain. I had a job to do.

I shifted into my suite, appearing directly behind Patrick where he'd sat at the table, but out of Lucinda's line of sight. Or at least that had been the plan. I always remembered exact dimensions of a room, having once stepped into it—like one of those oddballs on TV who never forgot anything. Except my ability only had to do with numbers and spaces and calculations. Everything else I forgot like the rest of the world.

Neither Patrick nor Lucinda was where I'd left them. Looked like Keene and I weren't the only ones taking advantage of some private time. They were wrapped in each other's arms in the double doorway between the bedroom and sitting room. Patrick swung out an arm to steady them as their lips parted.

I leapt up from the floor, one of my knives slipping into my hand. More numbers appeared in my head, though not as prominent as when Keene's synergy had been at work. My instincts warned me to shift away from the house altogether, but I wasn't leaving Patrick. When I could identify no immediate threat, my heart rate ratcheted down to a level that permitted me to push the numbers away from my seeking mind.

"Oh, Mari," Lucinda murmured. "I didn't hear you come in." Her gaze dropped to the black knife in my surprisingly steady hand.

Keene burst through the door, his gaze going first to me and then to Patrick. "Everyone's okay," I said.

Patrick stepped back from Lucinda but angled his body as if to shield her. "What's happening?"

"No one came in here?" Keene asked. "Nothing through the window?"

"No. What was that noise?"

"Small bomb came through the hall window." I hurried to the door, where Keene was already stepping back into the hallway. Patrick and Lucinda hurried after us.

The Secret Service agent was up, gun in hand, pushing his body against the wall to peer out the ruined window. He swore under his breath. "They found us."

"Who?" I asked.

A trickle of sweat came from his close-cropped brown hair, skidding down the middle of a forehead creased with stress. His cheek was bleeding from several cuts, probably made by the shattering glass. "Don't worry about it, ma'am. We have it covered." He pressed a button on the transmitter fastened to his lapel. "Everyone's okay up here." As he finished speaking, the black agent who'd led us to my suite earlier barreled up the stairs, gun drawn.

"Perimeter secure," he said, urging Patrick back into my suite. By his size, the man must have been a football player at one time, and he didn't seem averse to using his body in corralling us.

Stepping around him, I marched over the broken glass to the window, ignoring the disapproving stare of the agent there. "Please, miss, if you'll just stay back."

How annoying that he didn't know my true nature, couldn't know that he was in far more danger than I was. Ignoring the hand he placed on my forearm, I stole a glance out the window. I'd expected Hunters, but instead a handful of women with signs crowded on the sidewalk. They stared at the house in confused fascination.

Keene came after me, sending the agent by the window into more fits of scowling. "What do you bet one of them has Hunter connections?" Keene kept his voice low, for my ears only.

"Maybe it's time to find out." I started back down the hall.

"No, Mari." Keene stayed close as I entered my suite—too close. "The Secret Service will handle this."

"We need to know."

He sighed, his glance flicking to the bathroom that connected to my sitting room. "I'll cover for you."

"You watch Patrick." For the moment, at least, Patrick and Lucinda were fine, and the black Secret Serviceman, whose name I couldn't remember, looked ready to defend them with his life.

I headed to the bathroom, shifting the second I'd locked the door, appearing across the street in the shadow of the neighbor's house. Sirens now filled the air, and the women were moving into the street, looking around nervously.

One woman who carried an oddly-shaped duffel bag separated herself from the group and moved purposefully in my general direction, though I was sure she hadn't spotted me. I shifted again into the cover of a pine tree at the edge of the property. She dropped the sign proclaiming *Sex with me = Unbounded child,* and picked up speed. By the time she was level with me, she was running.

Shifting from cover to cover, I followed her as she cut through the neighbor's property. On the far side, where the property bordered another street, a white van waited at the curb, a vinyl Hunter symbol plastered on the side. A man opened the sliding door, motioning toward her. "Hurry, hurry!"

All my instincts begged me to intercept the woman. I still had my knives. I might be able to take them by surprise, or at least her, but my cover would be completely blown, and that meant I wouldn't be able to be there for the next attempt. They'd just send more.

No time, I thought. Stifling frustration, I contented myself by taking a video on my phone as the woman threw her bag into the van with a loud clunk and herself in after. Tires squealed on the pavement as they took off, the sliding door still gaping.

The sirens were louder now, strident and insistent. Many police cars by the sound, and I knew this area would soon be overrun, the plants perhaps damaged. Too bad because the garden was beautiful, despite the cover of winter that still shrouded the foliage.

I reached mentally for the numbers, not to take me back to the house, but to Cort. I appeared in a sitting room as luxurious as my suite at Patrick's mansion. Cort was alone in the room, Jace and Noah nowhere in sight.

"Hey, you're late," Cort said.

"My weapons?"

He immediately picked up on my tone. "What happened?"

"Bomb tossed through a window. We're all okay, but we'd better be prepared for more." I'd feel a lot better with my regular knives, and that gun they made me carry might come in handy.

He hefted an oversized duffel bag from the very red couch and tossed it to me. "Let me know if you need us."

"I will. But the police are there now. We're fine."

I shifted back to the house, spying not only the coordinates of the bathroom, but the combination of numbers that meant dark green. *Keene.* He was still close by, guarding the door.

I ran the water a bit before leaving the bathroom and dabbed at the skirt of my suit with a washcloth. Somewhere I had picked up a stain, and this gave me an excuse for having stayed inside the bathroom that long. "I'm afraid I'm going to have to change before we go to the school," I announced as I joined the others in the sitting room.

Patrick and the others looked at me blankly. "What?" I said, adjusting the heavy black duffel on my shoulder. Noticing it, Keene took the bag from me.

"I can have your secretary cancel, Mr. Mann," said the black Secret Serviceman from the door where he stood guard. "Or if you're still going, we'll need to call in backup until this is investigated. We have a counter-sniper team in place on the roof, but we'll want more agents for possible crowd control."

Secretary? That was the first I'd heard of Patrick having a secretary. One more person to check out. These agents at least seemed to be on the up-and-up.

"No, we'll go." Patrick gave me a smile. "I'll let the school know we'll be a little late."

"I'll call for backup then." The agent pulled out his phone and stepped into the hall.

Keene's arm brushed mine, sending a jolt of awareness through me. Not his ability, not the numbers and colors, which I suddenly craved, but just him. His glance at me was controlled. Contained.

That boy needed a little loosening up, and I had some excellent ideas on how to make that happen.

Later.

I thumbed on my phone and played the video, making sure the sound was muted, then passed it to Keene. He glanced across the room to where Patrick was talking quietly with Lucinda. "Let's get this to Stella, and to Cort and Jace. Better them than the police."

I had to agree.

He handed back my phone and pulled out his own. "Patrick already let our people know about the school visit, but I'll make sure they do another sweep in the area, just in case."

TWENTY MINUTES LATER WE LEFT FRUSTRATED REPORTERS without a story and unsatisfied police officers canvassing the neighborhood. Both groups had questioned, with no result, the sullen women outside the house, who were angry at being suspected of anything besides wanting to have Patrick's love child. The Secret Service had called in reinforcements and made sure no one followed us.

We'd all had to change, and now I wore the blue suit and skirt I'd unpacked less than an hour earlier. Keene, Patrick, and I were wearing wireless earbuds and microphones. My mics were embedded in my earrings. Keene and I were also fully armed with our regular weapons, and we made sure Patrick was too. After the explosion in the mansion, we weren't taking any chances.

Lucinda chattered nervously all the way to the grade

school, but as we approached, she spied more vehicles from the media waiting for us. "I can't do this," she whispered, her regal face paling and her voice becoming strangled. "Not even as only a friend." Her eyes locked onto Patrick's, as if she'd been cast adrift in an ocean and he was her only chance of rescue.

There seemed to be no women lining up outside the school to throw themselves at Patrick, or Hunters threatening to take him out, so it was difficult to understand why Lucinda seemed so paralyzed.

Patrick hit the limo's intercom. "Drive around the block again. Stop when I tell you. My fiancée's friend has decided not to join us. One of you needs to go with her for a while to make sure no one follows. Thank you."

"That's not necessary," Lucinda said. "I'll just walk around a bit. Maybe do a little shopping. Or go to my self-defense class that I'm missing this morning. I'll meet you back at the house."

For a moment Patrick looked ready to lean across the seat and gather her into his arms, but he remembered in time. "He'll follow you for a few minutes. Just in case. We have extras with us now anyway."

She nodded, an apologetic crease appearing between her brows. "I'm sorry."

"It's okay," he said. "It won't always be this way. When this is all over, we'll go away somewhere."

I hoped for their sake he was right. I didn't know what Lucinda thought, but "all over" was further away than I cared to think about for a man that was both the president's son *and* the only publicly known Unbounded.

After we let her off, and one of the agents in a car behind us emerged to follow her, Keene said quietly to Patrick, "So, Luce thinks we're Homeland Security." With all the excitement, I'd forgotten about that, but apparently it bothered Keene as well.

Patrick gave us a sheepish look, his wide mouth for once not smiling. "I'm not sure how she got that idea. I went to talk to my dad last night about the situation, and afterward I met her in the gardens at the house and told her about you guys. I guess she just assumed, but it's my fault. Talking about Unbounded, or even Renegades, makes her nervous, so I sort of avoid it."

"Talking about Unbounded makes her nervous?" That made *me* nervous. What did she have against Renegade Unbounded?

"It's complicated."

"We're listening," Keene said. "Because we need to be sure she's not a danger."

Patrick glanced down, blowing out an exasperated sigh. "She's not a danger." He brought his gaze back up to meet Keene's. "Okay, I'll tell you, but I don't want you saying anything to her. That guy, Cullen, who faked being me for that entire year? Well, he hurt Luce physically. It was bad. She left and broke up with him. But you know how Unbounded genes are. She ended up pregnant, and when she told him, he forced her to get an abortion. And I do mean forced." Anger made his tone sharp. "They didn't just kill the baby, they took it all out. Guess the Emporium wanted to be sure there wouldn't be any claims down the road. She'll never conceive again. They stole that from her. From us. I don't care for myself because I love Luce more than anything, but I know she mourns the children she'll never have. And the fact that she can't have *my* children. No matter what, I'm going to take care of her. She was hurt because of me. Because she loved me."

"We had no idea." I reached out and touched his hand, and Patrick clung to me.

Several long seconds passed as Patrick struggled for control, the honk of horns and engines from the traffic around us sounding loud in the quiet. "Took me hours to get her to listen when I came back, but eventually she did, with a little help from Noah and my father. We were happy in Europe until the announcement. Anyway, Luce may look weak, but she's really strong inside. She still has nightmares and sometimes she looks at me like she's remembering someone else, but she's a survivor. If she made it through all that, she can make it through anything. And I'm going to help her. I have a lot to make up for."

"It wasn't you," Keene reminded him. "You were every bit as much a victim."

"But *I* can still father children. And I can't forget that it was someone who looked exactly like me that did this to her. Look, I know my time with Luce will be comparatively short, but I'm going to do my best to make her life everything she wants. I take care of the bills, I'm encouraging her to get her masters, she has a therapist, and we enrolled her in self-defense classes so she won't feel so helpless. I think she's happy." His eyes took on a pleading look. "Maybe it's not necessary for her to know you two are Renegades. She realizes the Secret Service agents don't know you're undercover, but maybe exactly where you come from isn't important."

"I don't think it matters," I said.

Keene glanced out the window where we had once again pulled up outside the school building. "It's your decision." Disapproval filled his tone.

"A lot of people don't tell all the truth," I said pointedly. To Patrick, I added, "Go ahead and protect her. I would." I caught Keene's gaze and smiled. He blinked as if I'd taken him by surprise. Guess he thought I was holding a grudge, but now that I'd had time to think about it, I knew his choices made sense to him, even if they were wrong to me.

"Come on," I said. "Let's do this."

I started to open the door, but Secret Service was already there. Patrick emerged behind me, placing his arm around me and nodding to the reporters as the pictures began. There were more reporters now than there had been before we dropped off Lucinda, perhaps having decided the school visit was worth their time after news of this morning's attack hit the airwaves. The sky had lost its earlier gray, easing into a calming blue, pillowed by the occasional puffy cloud. A perfect, beautiful day to be alive, even in the midst of all the attention, or perhaps because of it.

The Secret Service rushed us inside. The hallways were clear, guarded by more Secret Service, and a large metal detector, now shoved against the wall, told me everyone had been checked for weapons. The school children weren't assembled in a gym as I'd expected, but in a large classroom—a kindergarten classroom by the looks of it. There were only about thirty children of varying ages, their faces representing every race living in the DC area. *So this is a photo op, not a real school assembly.* I'd bet there were as many Secret Service on the premises as children in this classroom. A video camera in the back of the room recorded everything, but only five reporters were present.

Two school officials met us as we entered the room. A dark-skinned woman of unidentifiable race, medium height, and close-cropped hair offered Patrick her hand. "Welcome. I'm Verlene Haskell, the principal here. Thank you so much for coming. The kids have talked about nothing else since we told them. But we agreed with the Secret Service to move things in here after what happened this morning. More containable. The rest of the kids are watching on closed-circuit TV in their individual classrooms. I really appreciate you making the time to show them a piece of history in person." Her words were firm and her expression unreadable like her ethnicity, but she had kind eyes that made me feel she was sincere.

After a quick introduction to her vice principle, Ms. Jeppson, a short, round woman with apple cheeks and a ready smile that didn't quite reach her hazel eyes, Ms. Haskell led Patrick and me to the front of the room. Keene stayed behind, scanning the group.

"Would you like to join us, Shelli?" Ms. Haskell said to a small girl who was in the corner near a large plastic kitchen. Shelli nodded, tossed something into a basket containing fake food, and found her seat.

Ms. Haskell presented us to the children, then indicated two chairs where we could sit as we addressed them. I slid into one, but Patrick remained standing, beginning his presentation in an animated voice with large gestures. The littlest students at the front were rapt, staring in wonder as he told about the Unbounded and what he hoped to see happen in the world. One little girl with short, wiry hair tamed into two pigtails came to sit on my lap. I nearly laughed in surprise, but I put my arms around her.

I glanced up to see Keene staring at me from the corner with the play kitchen, a wistful smile on his face. I knew what he felt. This was normal. Well, not the cameras or the Secret Service, but these children. The normal, everyday experience of going to school with a variety of kids was something he'd never experienced while growing up with the Emporium where he'd been trained so differently in just about everything.

He winked and heat rushed through me. For an instant, numbers representing both places and colors exploded in my vision. Then he bent down and picked something up from the basket of plastic food, breaking the connection. My arms tightened around the little girl.

As Patrick started wrapping up, my phone vibrated in the pocket of my jacket, and I was surprised to see that it was Cort. I slid the little girl off my lap and encouraged her to return to her seat. She gave me a small smile as she obeyed. The vibration on my phone stopped.

Patrick glanced at me but didn't miss a beat as I retreated to the hallway where two Secret Service officers we hadn't seen before stood guard, a tall, big-boned woman, and a man who was equally as tall but pole-thin. Keene joined me as I called Cort back.

"Can you talk?"

"Yeah, I'm with my *brother* and two Secret Service agents." I smiled at the agents, but they didn't look my way.

"Better connect Keene in then."

"Okay." I did as he asked. "He's on with us. What's up?"

"I know you have people listening, so I'll do all the talking. We've pinpointed a sniper on the roof of the building next to the school, well hidden from the counter-sniper unit."

A shiver ran through me. Something told me this was the last school Patrick was ever supposed to visit.

CHAPTER 10

I PACED DOWN THE HALL, GRATEFUL THE SECRET SERVICE DIDN'T follow me, though their eyes were on me now. Maybe if I stayed in sight they'd keep their distance.

"Stella did a thorough sweep of the cameras in the area," Cort continued, "and she can't identify any other reason for the man to be up there, unless he's gunning for Patrick. She's going through more data now, but he's been there since just after you arrived. No idea if it's connected to what happened at the house this morning, but we need you to stay inside the school until Jace can catch up to him."

"We can do that," I said.

Cort cleared his throat. "There is another concern. So far, all we turned up with that van you recorded this morning is an empty garage that was rented out last week. They paid cash. Our greatest concern is that the attack this morning shows desperation and a willingness to escalate. If we're right about the sniper, it's likely Patrick won't be the only target because a bullet won't kill him. The sniper's purpose will be to create enough distraction to get to him so they can finish the job."

Keene's strides as he paced around me were short, his body rigid. "There are more snipers then, or at least one more, and they'll shoot anything in sight. They'll also have a car with drivers to grab Patrick once he's down."

"That's our bet." Cort's voice was tight like Keene's pacing. "With so many Secret Service around, it'll have to be fast."

"The bystander casualties don't sound like Hunters, though," Keene said.

I stepped in front of Keene so he'd have to stop pacing. "Looks like mortals are evolving too. Survival of the fittest." No matter how any of us felt about it, the Hunters' idea of getting rid of all Unbounded would save the human race every bit as much as the Renegade plan to vanquish the Emporium.

"Needless to say," Cort said, "capturing the sniper and bringing him in for questioning would be a real break. Problem is, Jace is still some distance away, and the sniper will know something's up if Patrick doesn't come out soon. The guy already looks really nervous on the footage we have, and he may abandon his post. We have no idea where the other snipers may be, so even without him, they may accomplish their goal."

"I'll go," I said. "I can get to him in time, and make

him tell me where the others are. Keene can stay with Patrick." I almost expected someone to object, but no one did, though Keene didn't look too happy.

"Just be careful," Cort said. "I'm sending his coordinates to your phone, and several aerial photographs to help you orient yourself. But turn on your radio. I'll stay in contact with Keene, and he'll communicate with you, provided you stay in range."

"All right." I hung up and began looking for a bathroom where I could make the shift to the outside. I knew just the place, over by the playground slides. I could see the location in my mind and knew that none of the agents watching the outside of the school would see me there.

"Better tell Patrick to talk longer," I said to Keene. "Have him tell how he and I met, or something. Maybe how he and the president's biological son were switched at birth by the evil Emporium." I was mostly kidding about this last, because while much of the world knew Patrick had been switched, the Emporium's roll in that act had not been publicized.

"Mari," Keene began, his hand touching my arm and sliding down a few inches.

"I'll shift out if I need to." I wanted to urge him to use his ability to enhance mine. Maybe with that kind of power I could shift us both. But Patrick needed Keene here, and besides, Keene wouldn't risk blowing me up for something he knew I'd been trained for. I could do this alone.

"See you in a few." I ducked into the bathroom that

I'd finally found halfway back to the classroom, leaving Keene to tell Patrick to drag things out.

"Looks like I'm spending all my time in bathrooms these days," I muttered, kicking open a stall with a toilet that was smaller than normal and nearer to the ground.

I shifted before the door closed, appearing near the green tube slide. My GPS was already pointing the way, but instead, I studied Cort's photographs. Apparently, the man was on top of the building kitty-corner to the school, not directly across or next door. I couldn't see the top of the roof myself, just the wall around it, but the pictures showed me what was up there. All I had to do was put the two together in my mind and choose a number that would place me behind the structure that housed the stairs leading onto the roof—undoubtedly the best place for me to appear. There were other small structures on the roof, presumably for heat, air conditioning, and venting, and one of these looked like it blocked the sniper from being seen by the counter-sniper team. Someone in Secret Service hadn't been as careful as he should have been.

Pleasure swept through me as numbers came into focus. I wanted to laugh with the power of it. Even without Keene's ability, I felt as if I could do more than before, that I understood my gift as I hadn't earlier. But it was more promise than a full knowledge. I was looking forward to discovering the rest. I saw Cort's blue color number, far away, and what I was pretty sure was Jace's purple. He'd be excited that I could finally pinpoint him and would probably use it as another excuse to hit on me.

Then I was there, behind the structure I'd targeted. A cool breeze swept my hair away from my face, fresh air that made me feel alive, invigorated. Inching against the wall, I peered around it to see a man intent on the school grounds, staring through the scope of his rifle as the satellite photo had shown. I couldn't see much of him under the sweatshirt and baseball cap, but he was shaped like a block and short blond locks curled up over the edges of his hat.

I crouched and shifted close behind him, my metal blade slipping around to the front of his throat. "Drop it, Hunter," I growled.

He startled, his back bucking against my chest, but he let go of the rifle. I kicked it aside, digging the knife into his skin and forcing him to stay on his knees. "Careful now, you don't want me to slip, do you?"

A trickle of sweat dripped from under the hat, despite the refreshing breeze. "D-don't slip," he stuttered.

"You mean like you were going to slip on that trigger?" No response. "Where's the other man?" I asked.

His body stiffened, telling me we were right. "There's no one but me," he said, much too late.

"You're lying." I dragged the knife across his skin, not breaking it. Not yet. If I was truthful, a part of me was eager to cut him, to make him pay. He was like Trevor, after all. It scared me a little, my fascination with knives, the call they had for me. How easily I could hurt someone. "I'm going to ask you one more time and then I'm going to have a little fun with my knife." I could smell his fear, and I wasn't too sure that he hadn't wet himself. Nausea rose in my throat. No. I didn't want to hurt this man. I didn't have to give in to the knife's temptation. That wasn't me.

"Mari," Keene's voice said in my ear. "Jace is almost there, but they haven't located a sign of anyone else. We're thinking maybe we were wrong."

"Oh, there's another man. I'm sure of it."

The Hunter's eyes rolled up to look at me, blue with altogether too much white. He must think I was crazy talking to myself.

"Well, where?" Keene sounded impatient.

Withdrawing the knife, I shoved the Hunter around, my foot slamming into his chest as he twisted on his knees. He had high cheekbones, flushed now, and chiseled features that most women found handsome, but his mouth was small and mean, and his eyes full of hatred. I had no doubt he'd cut me in three as easily as he'd have pulled that trigger on Patrick. On the children.

The Hunter grabbed the straps of a duffel bag lying next to him and threw it at me as he lunged to his feet. His trajectory was good, and he would have hit me hard, maybe hard enough to drop the knife, but all the brute force in the world was useless against someone who wasn't there.

I reappeared at his side, pounding my right fist into his cheek. He dived for me again, and this time I let the hungry knife cut through the long sleeve of his T-shirt, digging deep. He screamed and grabbed at the wound as I hit into him again, knocking him to the ground. This time I pulled my compact pistol from the holster tucked inside the back of my skirt. I didn't know what it was about men that they feared guns more than knives. Knives could cause so much more pain. Slow death. Guns were far too quick. But whatever it took.

"Where's your buddy?" I put my foot on his chest, pinning him to the roof.

He sobbed and covered his head. "Don't shoot me. Don't shoot me!"

"What about the children?" I could almost see them in my mind, falling to the ground, roses of red blossoming on their small bodies. "You were going to hurt them."

"No! I promise!"

"I don't believe you." I leaned more weight on his chest as it bucked with his sobs. "Tell me where your friend is. I won't ask nicely again."

I heard a crunch on the rooftop behind me. "I'm right here."

I turned, spying a big man with a long, strawberry blond mane and so much facial hair, I couldn't see anything but blue eyes, a bit of pale cheeks, and a wide nose with huge nostrils. He was dressed in jeans and a navy-blue plaid shirt that probably would have been too large for Santa Claus. The gun in his hand was a lot bigger than my nine mil.

"Keene, I found him," I said.

The man squeezed his trigger.

CHAPTER 11

BURNING PAIN SLICED INTO MY UPPER ARM AS I REAPPEARED behind the big man. Fortunately, he was a lousy shot. Unfortunately, I hadn't shifted fast enough to avoid the bullet. Deep red poured down the powder blue of my right sleeve. My fingers lost their grip on my gun, and it clunked to the ground. Unlike with my knives, I wasn't nearly as good shooting with my left, so I didn't bother to pick it up. The big man started to turn.

"What's happening?" Keene shouted in my ear.

Ignoring him, I kicked hard, whipping around to jab my foot into the side of the Hunter's knee. He went down with a satisfying crunch, his weight working in my favor. But there was still his gun. I shifted to his other side as he tried to aim at me.

My arm felt numb now, as though my body was so overloaded on pain that it couldn't feel at all.

Good.

Lashing out with another right kick, I sent his gun clattering over the rooftop. He roared and lunged to his feet, his good knee holding his weight. I punched him hard in the stomach, but my blow bounced off without seeming to hurt him in the least.

Remind me not to pick a fight with Santa Claus, I thought.

Keene shouted in my ear, "Jace is almost there!"

"Shut up! I'm trying to concentrate." I was so going to thump him hard the next time I saw him.

The big Hunter kept coming, arms wide as if to crush me to death. I threw my larger knife from the sheath on my leg. The metal sang as it embedded into the softness of his belly. He howled and clutched at it. I had another knife ready, but he backed away, nearly collapsing when he stepped down on his bad knee.

"Run and I'll put this in the back of your neck," I threatened. The numbness in my arm was fading now. Lurking somewhere was an agony I knew I'd have to embrace sooner or later.

A noise made me shift instinctively. I appeared once more behind the big man, expecting to see the first sniper with a gun in his hand. Instead, it was Jace, a grin on his face that was almost happy. He stood over the first sniper, one gun pointed down at him and another at Santa Claus.

My shoulders sagged and the pain finally came— blinding, white hot. I bit my lip to keep from crying out.

"Sorry I didn't get here sooner," Jace said.

I reached for numbers, focusing on them to push back the pain. "I managed."

"Yeah. You barely saved any for me." He sounded disappointed.

I stepped closer to Santa Claus, who was trembling, his breath coming in gasps. He'd balled up his plaid shirt and was holding it against his wound, my knife still inside him. "They've seen me shift, and we have enough problems." Without mortals having proof of our abilities, I meant.

"We'll get them to Ava and Erin after we question them. They'll never remember meeting us." Jace's grin became sinister.

The big man didn't resist as I guided him to his knees and pushed my knife against the front of his neck. The sun glinted off the blade, turning it bright with promise. Ever beckoning. "Are there any more snipers?" I asked the Hunter.

"Oh, just kill him," Jace said. "I know how you love to play with your knives. I'll get the information from this one." He waved a gun over the sprawled man's heart.

Jace was bluffing, of course. We would kill them if we had to, but only in self-defense, not for information. Lucky for them, we weren't Emporium.

"One more!" huffed the big man. "Over . . . in that building. Third . . . window . . . on right." He flung out an arm before bringing his hand back to his stomach wound.

Jace scowled. "Great."

"You hear that?" I said to Keene. "Don't let Patrick leave." To Jace, I added, "I'll go."

"You have enough of a view to shift?" Jace looked doubtfully across the space that separated us from the apartment building.

I nodded. It'd be better if I knew the layout, but if I started to shift into a wall, I could change the number during the shift.

"What about your arm?" Jace asked.

I looked down. The bright red flow might have reduced somewhat as my increased metabolism rushed to repair the wound, but it'd be a few hours until I was really okay. A shot of curequick would help matters greatly. "I'll be fine. I won't stop to chit chat with him. But maybe you should keep questioning these guys. Just in case."

Again the evil grin. "My pleasure."

"I swear that's all," said the sprawled man next to Jace. "Please, my arm's bleeding an awful lot. Can I wrap my shirt around it?"

"Fine." Jace stepped back, still keeping guns on both men. Guns that he really didn't need. He could end both men with a few choice punches. But he wouldn't. I'd seen him lose the contents of his stomach after a fight, and while he hadn't done that in a while, death still affected him deeply. He enjoyed practicing his ability in a fair fight, and winning battles against Emporium agents, but he didn't enjoy hurting mortals, even Hunters.

"Mari, what does he mean about your arm?" Keene

said as I reached for the numbers that would put me inside the apartment with the sniper.

"Maybe next time you'll come along and find out." The reference to using our abilities together was kind of mean, but I kept my voice light because I wasn't angry at him. Just in a lot of pain. It would be better to let Jace go for the third guy, but it'd take him too long to get out of this building and inside that one, and now that the pain from my wound had hit, I doubted I could take care of these two alone unless he secured them first, and that would also take time. Every second that passed meant a greater chance of the last sniper getting trigger happy and someone outside that school dying.

Keene was silent for several heartbeats and then, "We'll talk about it later."

I shifted, appearing inside a small apartment.

I'd calculated ten feet from the window where I hoped the man would be. I had more numbers prepared that would take me five feet to the left and other coordinates that would take me even further away. There was no need.

A woman, not a man, knelt by the open window. She peered into the scope of her rifle. The lines of her body were rigid, determined. The apartment looked like a home. Maybe hers. She must have come and gone a million times to this place, and if that was the case, not even Stella could have pegged her as someone unusual. She wore headband earmuffs over her long brown hair so she didn't hear me shift in.

Replacing my knife in my arm sheath, I picked up

the lamp from a table and shifted closer to the woman, slamming it down against her temple. It wasn't elegant or pretty and there might be lasting damage, but it was efficient and I was feeling weak enough that it was all I could do. My left hand did have limits, and this was safer for the woman than my knives. I caught her as she fell, protecting her head from the wood floor. As I laid her down, I recognized her as the woman who fled after the bombing this morning at Patrick's house.

A wave of hot pain flooded my arm and blackness nibbled at the periphery of my vision. "Keene," I said. "We're clear, but I'm not sure I can make it back there now. I need time." I was a mess anyway. How could I step out of the bathroom at the school covered in blood and with my skirt ripped halfway up the side? And tomorrow I'd never be able to explain to the world how I, supposedly a mortal, healed from a gunshot wound overnight.

"You can't stay there."

"I may not have a choice." I slid to the floor. I'd been in several serious conflicts, but so far I'd been lucky not to get shot. I never dreamed there could be so much pain concentrated in a single spot. I didn't know how Ritter could continue to fight with multiple bullet wounds.

"Mari," Keene's voice was hard. "You need to get out of there now. Shift to the car. I'll figure out an excuse for the Secret Service. When Patrick leaves the school and no shots come, their friends waiting for the diversion are going to know something's up and will go searching for their people. Jace has his hands full. Cort's on his way, but he won't make it in time, and I have to stay with Patrick."

"I'll come in a bit. Give me a minute." The pain made my thoughts hazy. I just wanted to lie on the ground next to the unconscious woman and sleep for a week or two.

"Shift to the limo now! You remember the location, right?"

That made me find enough strength for a snort. "Of course."

"Do it now, or I *will* come and get you. Patrick be damned."

That got my attention. "Don't get your panties in a wad."

"I have your location on my GPS. If that doesn't change in five seconds, I'm coming for you."

"Okay!" I shouldn't have been surprised that he'd traced me. We all had tracking chips inside us, which in our line of work came in handy more often than not. Usually, I liked knowing my new "family" could always find me.

"Well?" Keene asked.

Numbers flickered inside my head. I could see Keene's dark green, and I wanted more than anything to shift to him and let him take it from there, but that would compromise Patrick. My fingers tightened around the woman's rifle, just in case her friends made it here before Cort did. "I'm shift—"

"—ing." I finished the word in my new location. But instead of the limo appearing around me, I found myself on the floor in another bathroom. A plush throw rug in front of the sink pillowed my head. It was huge as far as bathrooms were concerned, but I was sick to death of them.

"Mari, what are you doing?" Keene sounded angry now, his voice almost obscured by static.

"I don't know." I gave myself up to the darkness.

CHAPTER 12

THE SHARP JAB OF A NEEDLE AWOKE ME. PAIN FOLLOWED, just as stabbing and bright as the overhead lights. Keene knelt beside me, his lean face set. He pulled out the needle and inserted it again in another place and then another until all the liquid in the syringe was gone.

"That better be some kind of painkiller," I muttered.

"Mixed with curequick."

He put the needle aside and began cleaning my wound. Pain again rippled through me, but less now than before. I couldn't help the sigh that escaped my lips.

Keene chuckled. "Well, at least you came back to the house. I wasn't sure there for a minute until my GPS finally pinpointed your signal."

I was still lying on the bathroom floor, but there was a real pillow under my head now. A puffy white quilt I recognized as having been on my bed covered all of me but the arm, which lay on several equally white towels. The sleeve of my suit was gone, and the jagged edges told me Keene had cut it with a knife. He finished cleaning, and somehow the thread for stitches was already in his hands. I was happy he'd shot me with painkiller, but my body would get rid of it fast, so I hoped he hurried. I'd heal without the stitches, of course, but they would help the process. The curequick would also increase my already rapid ability to heal by up to five times.

Keene's hands were gentle, and for no reason at all I thought of how his hands had felt touching other places on my body earlier in his room. The door opened, scattering the thoughts, and Patrick slid inside, shutting the door behind him.

"Okay, I think we're good," Patrick said. "The Secret Service doesn't really believe your story about Mari leaving the bathroom without being seen, but since she's here and they believe nothing weird happened at the school, they're letting it go. They did post a couple extra agents here in case there's any more bombs." He knelt down next to me, smoothing my hair from my face where it blocked my vision. "I'm glad you're okay."

"Me too. But really, there wasn't much danger. I just moved a little too slow. Didn't know getting shot was this bad."

Patrick grimaced. "You never get used to it. When the Emporium had me, they used to shoot me just for fun. Then they'd fill me with their version of curequick so I'd recover faster and then do it all again." He shuddered.

"That experience is what made me volunteer to be the face of the Unbounded. We can't let the Emporium win."

"Too bad Hunters don't realize we're on their side," I said. "What about Lucinda? She okay?"

"She came back a while ago. She's downstairs in the kitchen now. The Secret Service agent who works with my cook is apparently out sick today, so Luce volunteered to help with what's going to be our very late lunch."

"Lucinda got past the reporters then."

"Actually, there aren't any. The Secret Service threatened to throw them in jail, so they finally left. But she came in through the garden anyway."

We were silent as Keene finished his stitches and began bandaging my arm. Already the effect of the painkiller was fading. "You got a pill or two I can take?" I asked Keene.

He smiled. "Not so tough now, eh?"

I rolled my eyes. "Contrary to what Ritter or Jace believe, there's no glory in suffering unnecessarily."

"The pills are here, but I'll grab a bottle of water from the bar in your sitting room." Keene gathered the supplies back into our industrial-sized first aid kit.

Patrick put his arm around me and helped me sit up. He kept holding me as Keene opened the door, but let his arm fall as Keene disappeared. "I love doing that," Patrick said with a chuckle.

"Doing what?"

"Touching you." He laughed again. "Every time I do, Keene bristles."

"He does not."

"He hides it well, but he does. I know I shouldn't enjoy torturing him, but I hate how suspicious he is of Luce, so it's kind of innocent payback. You don't mind, do you?"

I snorted. "I didn't even notice."

"I don't know what's going on between you two, but if you don't like him that way, you'd better let him know." Patrick's smile showed he knew that I *did* like Keene that way.

After the kiss in Keene's bedroom this morning, Patrick was probably right. What I didn't know was if it would be enough to help Keene overcome his fear of blowing me up. Because we couldn't have much of a relationship if he was too afraid to investigate his gift. If he wasn't willing to use it in our battle against the Emporium.

Then again, maybe he *would* blow me up if he gave in to me. It was a risk I was willing to take.

"Anyway," I said, returning to something Patrick said earlier, "he has a point about Luce. She wasn't there when this bloodbath would have gone down today. She skipped out. Now maybe that was because she was afraid of the media, but she wouldn't have been the focus of attention. It's almost like she knew something was going to happen."

"No way. Luce loves me."

But the quick way he said it told me he'd already considered it, or maybe Keene had forced it down his throat on the drive back.

"She wasn't there, Patrick. Do you believe in coincidence?"

His jaw jutted forward now, no trace of his usual smile. "I do because I know Luce. She's been a good sport about all of this. Despite her apparent relief at having you here, it's not easy for her to let another woman be my fiancée. To watch me kiss you on national TV."

"We still have to be careful and keep an eye on her. And on anyone else here. That reminds me. What's this about a secretary? Who's that?"

Now the wide smile was back. "Uh, yeah. Well, I did have a secretary at one point, but now I do everything on the Internet or through email. I have one of those neural headsets and with that I can take care of every communication in less than an hour—and there are a lot of them. Takes me less time than it did to tell my secretary what to do."

"That's believable. I've seen Stella at work." I rested my head against the cabinets behind me. "Who'd have figured that the most popular man in America right now does all his own appointments?"

"Most wanted man, you mean, and I'm not talking about those women." Patrick stood as we heard footsteps approaching.

"Those Hunters do seem out to get you."

Keene entered with a bottle of water, giving it to me with four pills. "Bottom's up. This should hold you for a bit." He leaned against the wall and stared down at me as I swallowed.

"We need to find out who's behind this," I said.

Keene folded his arms, looking thoughtful. "These aren't the actions of typical Hunters, so I'd say they're new ones, but I'd go so far to bet that they're being funded by the Emporium. That rifle you brought back with you isn't something even Hunters would have access to. Only the government or the Emporium would be able to get their hands on something like that in the first place, much less have them smuggled into the US."

"So you're saying the Emporium might want me dead, even though I'm working to get mortals to accept all Unbounded."

"That's exactly what I'm saying. I think their goal is to breed distrust and chaos until they come out on top and supposedly rescue the world. Cort's having Stella track the weapons Jace recovered. They're also going to send the Hunters back to Ava so she and Erin can look into their minds, but the Emporium has been at this a long time, and if they're using new Hunters, they may have covered their tracks. Until we hear from them, we need to sit tight and make sure no one gets to Patrick, even if we have to cancel his appearances." Keene was looking at me, but I knew he was speaking to Patrick.

"No!" Patrick protested. "I've got a schedule. Public opinion swings on a dime. I need to stay on this."

"Keene's right," I told Patrick. "So stop glaring at us and help us find the inside person."

"What if there is no inside person?"

"The Hunters always know where you'll be," I said.

"Uh, excuse me, but the press knows too. It's not a stretch to think this could all be coming from strangers who are watching my movements." Patrick paced two steps toward the door and back again, his strides jerky, his face worried.

"That girl got into the White House," Keene reminded him.

Patrick rolled his eyes. "A lot of people work there. No one got in here."

"Not yet," Keene said.

I was tired of both them and the conversation that was getting us nowhere. "I guess I'd better change." I'd prefer a nice hot shower, but it was simpler to wait until later tonight when the arm would be mostly healed.

Patrick hurried to help me rise, drawing his arm around me protectively. He winked when Keene couldn't see, and I pushed away from him. "Thanks, I'm okay." Both men followed me into my connecting bedroom. The bedroom door was closed to the sitting room, so at least I didn't have to worry about Lucinda or anyone else barging in.

"Wait," I said to Patrick as he started to the door. "Does Lucinda know what happened? Or that I was shot?"

He shook his head. "She's already nervous enough. I haven't told her anything."

"Good." I exchanged a glance with Keene, who now wore a hint of a smile on his lips.

Yes, it'd be a lot easier finding out whether or not

she was in on the sniper attempt if she wasn't told what had happened. Anything she might drop would help us nail her.

Patrick continued blithely to the door, unheeding of our exchanged looks. Keene waited until he was gone to say, "What if it is her?"

"Things aren't always what they seem. You know that." I walked into the closet and scanned the array of clothing Lucinda had finished hanging for me. I wanted jeans and a short-sleeved shirt that would be easy to pull over the bandage. I should use a sling to aid the healing process, but a jacket with a pocket would have to do to both cover the bandage and support my arm.

I felt for the pocket of my suit to remove my phone with my good hand, but the phone wasn't the only thing there. Nestled next to the phone was what felt like a piece of rubbery plastic. Withdrawing both items, I blinked curiously at the slice of fake bacon. I shook my head, a smile coming to my face. My little friend at the school must have left me a present.

Keene's chuckle made me look up. His grin was wide and knowing, and suddenly I remembered him bending over to pluck something out of the toy basket at the school. "You stole this from the school?" I asked as his laugh deepened.

"I wouldn't call it stealing exactly. More like borrowing. I'll send them a better set, if it makes you feel better."

I laughed with him, and the laughter eased all the ugliness of snipers ready to shoot school children dead on their own playground. Keene must have put the bacon in my pocket before I'd gone after the snipers. How, I wasn't sure. Maybe when we'd been whispering together in the hallway. It was sweet and silly and romantic. I loved him for it.

Loved him? My thoughts froze there and couldn't move on. After that horrible last day with Trevor, I'd believed I wouldn't love any man again. Opening your heart that way made you too vulnerable. But that was before I'd known I was Unbounded, that I had a destiny to help save humanity. That there were men like Cort and Jace and Dimitri and Ritter and Patrick who risked their lives and their own happiness to save people they didn't know.

"Thanks," I managed. Still holding the bacon and my phone, I awkwardly started unbuttoning my suit jacket.

"Need help?" Keene's smile became teasing.

"Actually, yes." There was no way I was going to be able to buckle those jeans or put on my shirt alone. I pulled a white blouse from the rack and tossed it at him.

"Okay then." Did he suddenly sound nervous?

Unbounded generally didn't think much of dressing in front of their comrades. Centuries of life and continuous ops where we had to sleep, eat, and dress in close quarters made nakedness lose its power. But I had only Changed four months ago, and while Keene had grown up inside the Emporium, three and a half decades did not equal centuries of experience. My heartbeat amplified as he stepped closer.

"Let your arms drop to your side and backwards a bit. Can your bad arm do that?"

Not comfortably, but I did it anyway. He eased my ruined jacket over my wound and the knives strapped to my wrists and let it slip to the floor. I wasn't sure whether I should be relieved or offended that he kept his gaze averted from the lacy, hot pink bra that I'd worn more in protest to the boring blah blue of that suit than because of its usefulness. Then he leaned closer, his chin brushing my cheek as he put the blouse behind me and lifted the short sleeves over my extended arms, pulling the material together in front. My heart banged against my chest. He began buttoning the blouse, and now his eyes were forced to graze the swell of my breasts. My heart pounded more furiously. Leaving the last three buttons undone, his gaze slid slowly up to meet mine, like silk over my bare skin. Heat rushed between us. Numbers appeared in my head, more brilliant for the energy escaping from him.

"So, what about the skirt?" His voice sounded like gravel, as his eyes dipped to rest on my parted lips.

I stepped away from him, removing the now-empty holster from the back of my skirt and placing it on a shelf. Next, my empty sheath on my right thigh joined it—the bigger knife left behind in the Hunter I'd hit on the roof. With a deft twist, I undid the button on the skirt with my good hand, letting it fall to the ground. Stepping out of it, I placed my phone and the bacon next to the sheath and reached for my chosen jeans, which, fortunately, were more modern than the blouse, and comfortable despite their huge price tag.

I pulled them up with a little shimmy that brought more heat to my face, but I couldn't do the button or zipper. Or put back on the holster and find a new gun from the duffel bag of weapons that sat on one of the shelves. Keene's arms slipped around me and deftly finished the job, filling the holster with one of his own guns. For the briefest second I leaned back into his chest, feeling warm and content and safe.

"Are you angry about this morning?" he said, so softly that it felt like a caress.

I turned to face him, his arms still loosely around me. A laugh bubbled in my throat. "Even with thousands of years ahead of us, there's not enough time to waste being angry."

His smile warmed me. For a moment I thought we were going to have a repeat of the kiss, and I was more than willing, but my big mouth got in the way. "We should practice together using your ability," I said.

His arms dropped. "Let's talk to Cort first."

"We don't need Cort."

"I don't want to hurt you!" His voice was almost vicious.

I rolled my eyes. "So much of our ability is instinct. You need to trust yourself. Trust us together." I plucked my phone and the bacon from the shelf, shoving the phone into my pocket, but keeping the toy hidden in my hand. I stepped closer to him, into his personal space so he would have no doubt what I meant. "We *are* good together, don't you think?"

The green of his eyes was dark with emotion. "Oh, yeah." His lips came closer to mine, brushing them once, softly.

"Trust yourself." I slid the bacon into his jacket pocket. Two could play the game. "You would never hurt me."

"I—"

Whatever Keene was going to say was lost as the door to my bedroom banged open. "Come quick!" Patrick shouted. "It's Luce. I think she's dying!"

CHAPTER 13

IN MY SITTING ROOM, LUCINDA WAS LYING ON ONE OF THE couches, her face flushed. Her breath came in shallow, rancid gasps, and vomit stains marred her gray pantsuit. Her hands clutched against her stomach as she moaned. The black Secret Service agent who'd been so protective this morning knelt in front of her, fumbling for her pulse. No other agents were in sight.

Keene took one look and hurried back into my bedroom. "I'll get the first aid kit."

"What happened?" I asked, rushing to Lucinda.

"I don't know," she panted. "I can't breathe. I felt dizzy all of a sudden. I threw up in the hallway." Her pale eyes were wide with fear.

Patrick sat next to her and pulled something from his pocket that I recognized immediately: a portable neural transmitter. He set the device over his ear, forming a wireless connection from his brain to his computers—wherever they were.

"It's poisoning," said the Secret Serviceman.

I wished I could remember his name. "How do you know?"

"Sudden symptoms, her clammy skin."

Patrick leaned close to Lucinda. "Did something bite you?"

"No." She gave a little sob and released her stomach, clinging to his hands instead. "I was just downstairs helping Susan with the food. I came up to tell you it was ready in the dining room. I—" She stopped talking, her eyes going wide. "Oh, no!"

"What?" Patrick demanded.

A sob shook Lucinda. "I tasted the chicken."

"We have to get her to the hospital!" Patrick's voice was panicked. His neural transmitter blinked rapidly.

"Please don't let me die, Patrick." Lucinda was choking now, as if every second put her closer to death.

"I won't. You're going to be fine." Patrick slid closer, taking her in his arms. "Luce, sweetie, I need you to calm down. Help is on the way. Just breathe slowly." Lucinda's only answer was her eyes rolling up in her head in unconsciousness, which might be the best thing for her at this point.

"Why was she helping with the food?" the Secret Service agent asked. If he was surprised to see Patrick holding Lucinda like a lover, he didn't show it.

"I don't know, Chance," Patrick's lip curled. "Maybe

it was because *your* agent didn't show up today to help my cook."

Special Agent Chance, I remembered. *That's his name.*

Agent Chance jumped to his feet, surprisingly nimble despite his bulk. "Our agent arrived before we left for the school." He spoke into his lapel transmitter, "Status check." No reply. "Hey, everyone okay down there?" Still no answer. Chance looked toward the door, his furrowed brow telegraphing his worry.

"Go check on them," Keene said, coming from the bedroom, the first aid kit in his hands.

The agent gave a shake of his head. "My first duty is to Mr. Mann."

"Go!" Patrick said. "I'll be fine."

Dropping the kit onto the couch, Keene withdrew a gun from the folds of his clothing and an ID badge. Chance reached for his own gun, his eyes angry.

"Easy," I said. "We're on your side." Somehow a knife was in my good left hand. I hoped this didn't go badly because I felt the agent was on Patrick's side.

"We're Homeland Security," Keene said, tossing him the badge. "We had intel there might be an internal problem. We'll take care of Mr. Mann. Go check on your men."

Chance looked to Patrick, who nodded, and relief replaced the anger. "Okay. I'll be back." He ran to the door. "Stay here. Lock the door."

Keene went back to digging through the first aid kit. I didn't get in the way. We had a lot available to us, and

Keene had been in the field longer than either Patrick or me. "It's poison all right," Keene said. "Snake or spider venom, most likely. But we don't know what kind so we need to act fast. I hope this antivenom works, or that she didn't get much."

"It needs to be a polyvalent antivenom," Patrick said, "or it may not do any good."

"You get that from the Internet?" Keene's voice was slightly mocking. "Well, that's standard issue, but I don't know how much to give her. She could go into shock."

"Here, let me." Patrick grabbed the large syringe, which had divisions inside for at least three different drugs. "I have the amounts . . . from the Internet." No retaliating anger came with the comment. Tears wet his face as he pushed up her sleeve.

"I'm going to see what's happening downstairs." I reached for the numbers that would place me in the main hallway.

"First get Patrick an assault rifle," Keene said.

I shifted to the closet near my duffel of weapons and returned in seconds, placing the rifle beside Patrick on the couch.

"I'm going with you." Keene jumped toward the door. "Lock the door after me. Then come." To Patrick, he added. "We'll be right back. Don't open the door to anyone. If they try to break in, shoot them."

I sprinted to the door and locked it before shifting to the hall on the main floor. Keene came flying down the stairs to join me before I could reach the kitchen. Energy crackled all around him, and I knew he'd been using his synergy to increase his own speed. *Interesting.*

In the kitchen we found Special Agent Chance standing with his gun aimed at Susan, who paid no attention. Her face was fixed in horror at three Secret Service agents, two of whom had collapsed on the floor. The third was still in his chair but sprawled against the wall.

"What did you give them?" Chance shouted at the cook. He glanced over at us, his eyes deadly.

Susan cringed. "Nothing. I swear! It was just chicken. I don't know how this happened!" She fell to her knees, her eyes glazed. "Are they dead? Oh, dear God, don't let them be dead!" Her head dropped to her hands as she started to sob.

"We need more antivenom," Keene said.

I shifted back upstairs and returned in time to see Agent Chance yank Susan to her feet. Neither of them noticed me. "What did you do with our agent? Where is she?"

"I don't know. I don't know! She left!"

"She wouldn't abandon her job." Chance shoved her into a chair and began throwing open cupboards and pantries. How did even such a large kitchen have so many?

Susan's head suddenly jerked upright. "But *you* have abandoned your job. You're supposed to protect Patrick! Why aren't you with him?"

Chance's head whipped toward us. "He's fine," I said

quickly. "The door's locked and he has an assault rifle that he's trained to use. But Lucinda's bad off."

Keene was injecting the fallen men. "I have no idea if this is going to work. Why isn't that ambulance here yet?"

"Someone called?" Chance said before disappearing into a pantry.

"Yes," I said. By now Patrick had used his connection with his network to alert Cort, Stella, the White House, and probably every hospital in DC.

Chance emerged from the pantry, carrying a woman I'd never seen before, now wrapped in his own dark jacket. Susan glanced up and gasped. "Is she—"

"Dead," Chance confirmed. "Looks like she was hit with something heavy from behind, and then stabbed." He laid her gently on the floor by the other agents. Taking cuffs from his pockets, he grabbed Susan roughly, shoving her to the ground and forcing her arms behind her back. "You're gonna pay for this."

"I didn't do anything!" Susan cried.

"If you didn't, we'll sort it out." I gave Agent Chance a stern look. "Don't hurt her." To Keene I added, "Come on. We can't do anymore for them. Let's get back to Patrick." He followed me out the door, and I shifted as he did. Upstairs, I unlocked the door for him and went back to the couch. Lucinda was rasping as she struggled to breathe.

Patrick gazed up at me, his face stricken. "She came to for a second. I think she's dying. Please, isn't there anything you can do?"

Keene entered the room, and I said to him, "We have to get her to the hospital now."

He knew what I was asking. "And how are we going to do that? You've never been to any of these hospitals."

"Dimitri then. If you'll help maybe I can—"

"Maybe!" The word was practically a shout. "You want to go clear across the country when we haven't tested it? We might end up in the desert or an ocean."

"It's folding space. It doesn't work like that."

"We don't know how it works. I could—"

"Blow us all up. *I know.* But you won't." I waved his next protest aside. "Cort then. He's nearby and his ability will tell us how the drugs are reacting with her system."

Keene still hesitated. "Please," Patrick said. "I can't lose her."

Keene nodded, and I reached out, searching for the numbers. Those that signified Cort's blue popped into my mind, and also Jace's purple. Noah was a dark shade of pink. They were close together, and on our street where I'd expected them to be. "Okay, do your thing," I told Keene. "Patrick, tell Cort we're coming." Patrick's neural transmitter began blinking.

Keene's synergy poured into me, exciting my ability. Numbers came more clearly into focus. I saw Patrick's color and this time noted it was a shade of orange like Stella's, which made sense, in a way, since they were both technopaths. Lucinda was white, edged with a silvery gray, as though the poison was eating at her inner pureness.

Energy crackled through me, but I didn't feel full or as

powerful as I had in Keene's room. "More!" I told Keene, realizing that he was holding back. I reached out with my right hand and touched him, pain arcing through my wounded arm.

Numbers flared bright with color. Power flooded me, stealing my breath. Unlike in the limo, I was prepared for the sensation and directed my body to absorb oxygen. Keene's ability actually increased my absorption until I felt strong and alive. Power pulsed with every heartbeat, bringing a high I didn't ever want to end.

The air before us seemed to split, revealing a shimmering room equally as opulent as the one we were in. A glance at Keene's face showed concentration, his eyes dark with emotion I couldn't read. Whether he was working to sustain the power or to hold back some explosion that would send us into space, I could only guess. Unsure how it would work, I bent over to touch Patrick, who was holding tightly onto Lucinda.

I didn't so much step into as I pulled the room toward us. A thrill echoed through me. *Well, here goes nothing.*

I only hoped we'd all end up where we were supposed to be.

CHAPTER 14

THE GRAY OF THE *IN BETWEEN* NEVER REGISTERED IN MY MIND. I was simply there in the new place—and so were the others. I looked at Keene's astonished face and laughed. He'd been expecting trouble.

"We did it!" I took a step toward him—and my knees promptly gave out. Keene's hand tightened on mine and pulled me close. I felt spent, as if I'd run a marathon, but euphoric. I'd certainly won that race.

Except it wasn't over yet. Patrick had fallen onto the gray carpet with Lucinda in his arms, and now she was convulsing. Cort quickly overcame his astonishment at our success and fell to his knees by Lucinda's side. On a big wall screen Dimitri peered down at us from the conference room in San Diego.

"Whatever you gave her isn't working," Cort said. "The necessary interaction with the poison isn't happening. That means it was the wrong antivenom."

Dimitri nodded. "You need to hurry, or she'll have too much damage to her kidneys and other organs. I can fix some of that, but not if they're too far gone."

Cort held up a handful of syringes that he pulled from a first aid kit even larger than the one Keene had left behind. He rattled off several drug names. "I won't know which combination will work until I get it in her. Suggestions?"

"I believe I've seen this before in Russia," Dimitri said.

Dimitri's next words were lost to me as Keene whispered near my ear, "I'd better help." I nodded and he released me, going to kneel next to his brother.

A tug at my elbow distracted my attention from their urgency. "Oh, Jace," I said.

"Come sit down with me over here. Let them do what they can. You look spent. Man, I can't believe you managed to bring them all here. How cool is that? Cort just about had a heart attack when Patrick told us what you were doing. He thought you'd end up in a million pieces somewhere. For the record, I knew you'd be okay." He blew out a whistling breath. "Erin is going to go crazy when she hears. *I'm* going crazy! This is the coolest thing since, well, since I Changed."

I was torn between wanting to bask in my own amazement and wanting to help with Lucinda. But there was nothing I could do for her, so I let Jace show me to the red couch I'd seen before when I'd come to get our weapons.

The elegant house was warm, but I felt chilled. "If we don't get the right mix soon, those agents at Patrick's are all going to die."

"We'll get it to them," Jace said.

Keene and Cort had begun injecting Lucinda with drugs. She was no longer convulsing, but I didn't know if it was because of something they'd done or if she'd stopped on her own. When the scream of ambulance sirens finally cut through the quiet of the room. I felt relief that at least someone would be looking at those Secret Service agents.

Somewhere a door slammed, and Noah hurried into the room. Today she wore a summery, knee-length dress in a floral pattern topped by a short, light blue jean jacket. Her hair lay free around her shoulders in tiny tight curls that emphasized the delicate lines of her face. Her eyes skimmed over us as she hurried to Patrick's side. "How is she?"

"Doing better now, I think," Cort answered. He sat on his heels, holding a needle in Lucinda's vein. "Maybe just a bit more." He nodded at Keene. "Yours too. Slowly. I'll tell you when to stop."

Noah went to her knees, a hand on Patrick's shoulder. "It's going to be all right." Her voice was almost sing-song, as though she felt the need to comfort him with her music.

Patrick took his hand from Lucinda's cheek and clasped Noah's. Together their hands made a startling contrast of white and black. "Thank you," he said with a sigh. Noah nodded and kept hold of his hand. Patrick's features relaxed for the first time since Lucinda's attack.

Jace nudged me, and I was glad he was seated on my left, away from my hurt arm. "She's totally gone on him, you know."

I stared. "Noah? On Patrick?"

"Yep. Isn't that how women say it? Totally and completely gone on him. That's the real reason she didn't want to pretend to be his fiancée. Well, besides the fact that she's just not very good at defense. Or offense. Or fencing." He gave me a wink and a tentative smile that I returned.

I appreciated his attempt at lightening the situation. "He doesn't see her that way, and he won't. Not with Lucinda around."

"She knows that. She just wants him to be happy. She's lived several centuries already. They have time."

Time. Time for Lucinda to die and for Patrick to recover and go on. Still, it was an unselfish thing to do, staying in the background, and I found myself admiring Noah even more for it.

Jace made a face. "Weird, huh? I guess when it comes to relationships, I'm too young to look at them in anything but the mortal way."

So was I. Waiting didn't seem to be in my vocabulary. *Keene's Unbounded.* The thought rushed through me like a comforting autumn breeze. *I won't have to watch him age and die.*

I realized then that it did make a difference that he was Unbounded. Not because I felt any less attracted to him when he was mortal, but because now I could allow myself to care more because I didn't have to worry as much about losing him. Seeing Trevor repeatedly in my dreams, his throat slashed by the Emporium, had taught me the value of life.

"You know what this means, don't you?" The seriousness of Keene's tone pulled my attention back across the room.

"Yes," Cort said. "The Emporium is behind this."

Jace jumped up from the couch and paced in their direction. "How do you figure?"

"First the sniper rifles," Keene said, "And now because of the toxin used. Not something the average antivenom could counteract. Hunters may be determined, but so far they have mostly just tried to shoot us and then cut us apart. They have no clue that we typically carry antivenom or what kind of toxin to use to get around that."

"But the Emporium would know poison couldn't kill Patrick, if that's who they were trying for," Jace said. "I mean, it might, but he'd just regenerate."

"Exactly. It was only intended to immobilize." Keene tossed a handful of spent syringes into the first aid kit. "That means they'll be going to the house to clean up. We have to get back there now."

I rose and stood next to Jace, already reaching mentally for the numbers. Was it easier now? I thought it might be. The more I practiced, the more naturally shifting came to me, but this last time with Keene seemed to have taught me more in one shift than a dozen on my own, despite the accompanying exhaustion.

"Just a moment more. You'll need all of us." Cort finished an injection. "Okay now. The drugs seem to be counteracting the poison nicely." He stood and glanced at the screen where Dimitri still watched silently. "Thank you, my friend. Without your suggestions, I probably would have killed her before I got the right combination."

Dimitri inclined his head. "Deaths like that happen more than you want to know. But she needs further medical attention. If you're going up against the Emporium, you better get her to a hospital. Write down the meds we used."

"Good idea." Cort hurried to a small table, pulled a pad of paper from a drawer, and began writing.

"I'll take her to the emergency room," Noah said.

Patrick began gathering Lucinda in his arms. "I want to go too."

"Too risky." Keene shook his head. "You'll be recognized, and we can't protect you. Better stay here. We have no idea what we'll be facing at your house, and we need to get back to see what we can do for the Secret Service agents."

I was glad everyone agreed on that. Because the Emporium certainly wouldn't be worried about the fallen agents, except maybe to help them into the next world with a knife across the throat.

Patrick's jaw firmed. "I'm not leaving her. I'll wear a disguise. No one will know. Besides I'm armed."

"So am I," Noah said.

"As if that helps," Jace mumbled under his breath.

Patrick motioned to me. "Mari and Keene can join us as soon as you finish at the house. Or isn't that the way it works?"

Everyone looked in my direction, waiting. Because that wasn't the way it *had* worked previously. I couldn't shift to a place I'd never been before unless I knew someone there really well, and neither Noah nor Patrick should qualify. But that was before Keene had enhanced my ability. I knew Patrick's color number now, even without Keene's help.

"Yes," I said. "I can find him."

"She can take us back to the house and then join him in the car on the way to the hospital," Keene said.

Shifting to a moving car would be difficult, if not impossible, but I could wait for a traffic light. There were enough of them in DC and the traffic often forced everything to a torturous crawl. I should have been happy at Keene's trust that I could protect Patrick alone, but it seemed more like getting me out of the way. Still, Patrick was my job, so I'd choose not to take offense.

Cort said to his brother, "And you can go with her if it's not bad at the house. Let's go."

"Patrick?" Lucinda opened her eyes.

"Right here, sweetie," Patrick soothed. "You're going to be just fine."

Keene came close to me, his hand on my right elbow. Jace grabbed my left elbow and Cort my left shoulder. Everyone held their weapons ready.

Power filled my body as Keene's synergy enveloped me. For an instant, the euphoria was almost too much, but after a few moments, my brain adjusted. Some part of me was aware of Noah opening a suitcase full of makeup, wigs, and other disguise options and plopping a long blonde wig onto Patrick's head. "You can do the rest in the car," she said, her voice faint to my ears.

"Where shall I take us?" I asked.

"The stairs off the main hallway." Keene spoke without hesitation.

No sooner spoken than the stairs shimmered in front of us, looking like a desert mirage. I pulled it toward us.

"Awesome," Jace murmured.

As we shifted, I saw Patrick carrying Lucinda to the door.

CHAPTER 15

SHOUTS AND THE *WHOOSH!* OF SILENCED GUNSHOTS WARNED us immediately that someone else was in the mansion. The blast of an unsilenced shot from the kitchen sounded too loud in my ears.

Keene kept hold of my arm, his ability still active, which was a good thing because I felt as if I'd been hiking up Mount Everest for two days straight. "Looks like Agent Chance is holding out in the kitchen," he whispered. "You guys take them from behind. Mari and I will protect the agents."

His power flared, threatening to suffocate me until I remembered to absorb oxygen instead of trying to use my lungs. Then I was soaring on an impossible high, the exhaustion fleeing. For the briefest second, the coordinates in Venezuela appeared in my mind. I pushed them aside and shifted us to the kitchen instead.

We appeared in front of the stove, ten feet from where Special Agent Chance crouched behind an overturned table near the door leading to the hallway. With him was Susan, the cook. Next to the back door were four EMTs, three working on the fallen agents, and one with a gun pointed at the heavy back door, which was shut and locked tight.

Chance's head and gun whirled in our direction. "We're here to help!" I said, raising my hands, one of which held the gun Keene had given me in the bedroom. I couldn't reach very high because of my wound, but it showed our intentions. "We brought backup."

"How'd you get in here?" cried the EMT with the gun, now aimed at us.

"Point your weapon at the door!" Chance roared. To us, he added, "Mr. Mann?"

"He's safe."

The agent practically wilted. He was bleeding from at least two different gunshot wounds, and from the amount of blood, it was a miracle he was still conscious. "They came from two sides," he said. "I managed to shut the back safety door, and the bars and bulletproof glass on the windows have held so far, but I don't know how much longer I can prevent them from coming in."

"You've done great." I grabbed a food trolley and moved it in front of me for cover. Or maybe it was more for support, because without Keene's synergy, my strength had vanished again. I sank to a crouch.

Keene hurried to the EMTs, tossing down a large package of drugs he'd brought from the other house. He handed one of the men a piece of paper. "This is what they need. And how much. Well, actually that was for a woman who weighs a hundred and thirty or forty. We may have to give them more."

A volley of bullets shattered the kitchen door, the hits themselves louder than the bullets. One of the EMTs sobbed in fear. We glimpsed someone through the gaping holes, and Susan fired a gun at them, her face stiff and frightened. I hadn't known she was armed, but apparently Agent Chance no longer thought her responsible for the poisoning.

But if she wasn't working for the Emporium, then who was?

The rest of the door fell from its hinges, and I glimpsed an Emporium hit team of at least four. They came toward us firing their silenced weapons, and we blasted back with our unsilenced ones. The smell of gunpowder and smoke filled my lungs, choking me. My ears rang. Two Emporium agents fell toward us through the doorway, hit in front and from behind with bullets. That meant Jace and Cort were doing their job. The other two Emporium operatives had disappeared from my view. I hoped they were out of the game for good.

"Hold your fire!" came a shout that I recognized as coming from Jace.

"Hold fire!" I repeated to the others. "That's our man."

We stopped shooting and watched as Jace came into the kitchen pushing an unarmed man ahead of him. "We got all of them out there. Cort's just tying up the last—"

His words were drowned in an explosion that rocked the back door, sending it and one of the EMTs flying across the room. I shifted to get out of the way. Instinctively. Faster than I ever had before. *Thank you, Keene.* He wasn't helping me now, but I'd learned something from before. Shifting had become more than breathing; it was like the beating of my heart.

I reappeared outside in the garden, behind a pair of Emporium agents, one who was about to throw a grenade inside the kitchen. I lifted my gun and fired four times, two for each, ignoring the fiery pain in my right arm. They both went down.

I guess guns had their uses.

Keene was on top of them in an instant, checking each pulse before coming to me.

"You saved my life," I said, letting him peel my fingers from the pistol.

"What? You just saved the day, not me. I didn't do anything."

"Yes, you did. I have more control now. More . . ." It seemed stupid to say power, but that's what it felt like. "Whatever you did with your ability, it's a part of me now. I learned from it."

Keene laughed. "So I didn't blow us up."

"And I didn't send us to Timbuktu."

His hand went to my back, and all my senses urged me to step closer, to *do* something about his proximity. *Just adrenaline,* I told myself. If my adrenaline hadn't kicked in, I probably would have fainted from all the expended effort. "Come on," I said. "Let's help sweep the house. You can give me back my gun now. Er, your gun."

Minutes later, we were sure no one else was there, mostly due to the lack of shooting. The house was so large that searching it thoroughly would have required more time than we had. I was still anxious that more Emporium agents might show up, so we headed outside, using a side door that would keep us from the prying eyes of neighbors who must have heard the shooting and the explosion.

Something prevented my pistol from entering my holster completely, and investigation had my fingers scraping the rubbery bacon toy. I almost laughed out loud, but Keene's eyes were on me, so I palmed the toy calmly and slid the gun into place. When had he put it there? Maybe when he'd joined me in searching the house. I distinctly remembered him touching my back.

"Perimeter secure," Jace called from the garden. "No sign of more Emporium agents." He put on the speed and was at my side in an instant. "You okay? Nice shooting, by the way. Ritter would be proud."

"Ritter proud of my shooting? That really would be a miracle."

"We'd better get to Patrick," Keene said. He looked at Jace and added, "You got it from here?"

Jace nodded, his hair glistening gold in the sunlight. "Cort and the EMTs are finished with the Secret Service agents, though that Secret Service agent had to threaten the EMTs with his gun to get them to use our drugs. The patients should be ready to transport soon. The ambulances are still out front. The Emporium didn't touch them."

"You'll have to get out of here fast," I told Jace. "The Emporium will send more."

Jace gave an elaborate shrug. "We'll be okay. Someone called the police. Hear those sirens?"

I did now, though I hadn't before. Jace's combat ability made his senses better than most.

Jace continued with a grin, "Cort made a call to the Secret Service to come as well, just in case the police here have Emporium spies within their department. But we've told everyone that Patrick is in a secure location, so I doubt the Emporium will send more men. Cort and I are about to make ourselves scarce. You'd better report in once Patrick really is secure. No doubt they'll want to bury him under more Secret Service."

"No way," I said. "We can't have more deaths on our hands. Look at those men in there."

Jace's levity disappeared. "I agree. I don't know if they'll make it."

The woman Agent Chance had found in the pantry was already dead, but I didn't know where her body was now or who had killed her. Maybe one of the poisoned agents was working for Hunters or the Emporium. At this point, nothing would surprise me. The Emporium didn't care about rewarding mortals even for their loyalty, any more than they felt inclined to reward a stray dog they'd sent on a suicide mission.

"Well, have fun," I said to Jace, mentally pinpointing Patrick's location.

His grin was back. "Isn't that what we've been doing?"

I rolled my eyes. Patrick's location wasn't changing, so I hoped that meant they'd gotten Lucinda to a hospital. I fished out my cell and texted him to see if he was alone. No response. "Patrick's not responding to tell me if it's safe to shift there. Maybe he's busy with Lucinda."

"What about Noah?" Keene said.

I nodded. "She's nearby. Not with Patrick but close."

"I have her cell number." Jace pulled out his phone and texted faster than I could follow with my eyes. After a few seconds, he said, "She's clear."

I nodded at Keene, taking his hand, and the increased clarity of my numbers was notable. I might have eventually learned enough to shift someone without Keene's help, but I wouldn't be able to do it now, not with how weak I felt.

We appeared close to Noah, almost materializing inside a grouping of chairs, until I changed numbers at the last moment. She blinked at us as we turned up on her other side instead. "Wow, that takes some getting used to."

"How is she?" We were in a waiting room of some type, with a TV blaring and surveillance cameras whose footage I'd have to ask Patrick or Stella to track down so we could erase evidence of my shift.

Noah frowned. "If all that lovey-dovey jabbering on the way here was any indication, Luce is going to be just fine. She even felt well enough to respond to a few texts."

"I'd better get to Patrick." I started for the door.

"They won't let you." Noah sank into the chair behind her. "Only family."

"I'm his fiancée."

"Actually, he said he was *her* fiancé. It was the only way they'd let him go back with her."

Right. Lucinda was the patient not Patrick. "I'll shift to him then."

"He should be right back." Noah glanced at the time on her phone. "She was really worried about going by herself. It's the only reason he even went with her."

A tingling of unease hit me. "She's safe now and feeling better, but she still wanted him to go with her? That's odd. She'd know it's safer for him to stay with you." I glanced at Keene, feeling suddenly nauseated at the suspicion crawling into my mind.

Noah nodded. "Yeah, but no one knows we're here. I thought it was safe."

I reached for Patrick's location as I said, "Susan was firing at the Emporium back at Patrick's. She didn't poison anyone. And it certainly wasn't Agent Chance, and everyone else is unconscious. Something doesn't add up."

"Lucinda," Keene whispered.

My thoughts exactly.

Noah didn't have much combat practicality, but she understood what we were saying. "No, not her. Luce loves Patrick."

"Then a tracking device or something. Or maybe Patrick and Lucinda were followed to Europe. We need to get to Patrick now." Keene took my hand, his synergy pushing me. "Go!"

I shook my head, panic flooding into my speech. "I can't find Patrick. He's vanished!" I didn't see how it was possible. I was the only Unbounded I knew with the ability to shift, much less take someone with me. He couldn't be gone that fast. I had the horrible feeling that Patrick's missing signal might mean he was already dead.

"Here I'll give you—" More intensity leaked from Keene. I felt dizzy, sick, ready to fly to not one but maybe a billion different locations. At the same time.

I squeezed his hand. "Stop, or you really are going to blow me up." I tried to keep my voice light, but I felt I was only holding my atoms together through sheer will.

Keene nodded and the pressure backed off. "Keep it ready, though," I added. Once more, I searched for Patrick's number among the many that filled my mind. Nothing.

"He's not here in the hospital. Or anywhere nearby."

"But he was just here!" Noah catapulted from her chair. Her hand went inside her jacket, reaching for her gun.

"Wait. I see Lucinda." That white with the dark edges

stood out clearly. I pulled her numbers closer. "She's still in the hospital, I believe. Maybe a different wing. And she's moving. Or someone's moving her."

"Could something be blocking you from Patrick?" Keene said. "Like how the electrical grid at the Fortress prevents you from shifting outside when it's on?"

"You mean maybe the hospital equipment?" His words gave me hope.

"I was thinking something more along the lines of the Emporium."

"Either way, he might still be here, and Lucinda should know what happened. We'd better alert Jace and Cort."

Keene raised the cell phone in his hand. "Just sent the emergency signal. They'll be tracking us."

His synergy flared again, and with his help, I pulled Lucinda's numbers towards us. An image rippled into existence. I blinked to see Lucinda walking alone, if somewhat shakily, down a hallway. Her gray pantsuit was rumpled and her short hair was tangled worse than when I'd seen her last. She looked dazed but determined as she placed one foot in front of the other.

"Let's go!" Noah urged.

I was tempted to leave Noah behind, but something definitely wasn't right here, and although she wasn't good at combat, she was trained. We had no clue if we were going up against just Lucinda, Hunters, or the Emporium, but one more body might mean the difference in a battle for Patrick's life.

"Okay." I dipped my head toward Keene, slipping my arm around him, mostly to ease the plastic bacon into his back pocket. We could be facing more than we could handle, and just in case, I wanted him to have it. I hated the possibility of never knowing how our game might end. "I'm ready."

Power rushed through my body as I folded Lucinda's location around us.

CHAPTER 16

A GLANCE UP AND DOWN THE HALLWAY TOLD ME LUCINDA was alone. Yellow caution tape blocked off one end of the hall, but I couldn't tell if that was to keep people out of this area or from crossing into the next. I still couldn't see Patrick's location.

Lucinda's back was toward us when we appeared, but she rotated unsteadily as she heard our arrival. One hand went out to the wall for support. "How did you get here?" she demanded sharply.

"Where's Patrick?" Noah asked. "Why are you out of bed?"

Lucinda's nostrils flared. "He doesn't need you anymore. Any of you."

"Who has him?" Noah flew across the ten feet separating us from Lucinda. She placed her hands on the taller woman's shoulders and looked into her eyes. "Please!"

"Has him?" Lucinda gave an unladylike snort. "Like I'd tell you anything."

Noah's arms dropped. "But I'm your friend—and Patrick's."

"Patrick's. Yeah, right." Lucinda's jaw thrust out. "I know all about your *friendship*. Mooning over him until I grow old and die and he turns to you for comfort. Tempting him, seducing him, with your voice. Stealing all his attention—and that of everyone else who listens to you sing. Not the kind of friendship I need."

"You have it all wrong," Noah said, pain evident in her voice. "I'm the one who urged him to go to you when everyone else said to let you go. Please, Luce, think of Patrick. He loves you."

"I *am* thinking of Patrick!" Lucinda continued to glare at Noah. "I'm *only* thinking of him! You don't deny it, do you? That you're in love with him?"

"Lucinda." I took several steps toward them, feeling as if my legs weighed seventy pounds each. *Shifting too many people in too short of time.* I should be helping Keene, who was opening doors near us and peering inside, but for now I'd have to leave it to him. Besides, I was sure that Lucinda was the key to everything. "We went back to the house, and Emporium agents were there looking for Patrick. They tried to kill everyone. And there were snipers at the school today. Their guns weren't something ordinary people can buy. Not even Hunters. Whatever these people told you, that's their plan—to kill him."

"She knows that." Keene's chin lifted in challenge, his hand pausing on the next doorknob. "Don't you, Lucinda? You didn't go to the school today because you knew about the attack. When it didn't succeed, you killed the agent in the kitchen so you could put the poison in the food."

"Luce?" Noah's eyes beseeched hers. "It's not true, is it? You were poisoned yourself."

"She didn't think it would happen that fast," Keene continued. "Not until we all ate it. She didn't know I planned to check our food." To Lucinda, he added, "I bet they said they'd give you an antidote." A flash of something in Lucinda's face told us he'd guessed right.

Noah's hand came up over her mouth. "Oh, Luce, no. They weren't going to. They never do! The Emporium doesn't care about mortals. What have you done? I know you love Patrick."

"You know nothing!" Lucinda's voice rose to a screech.

Noah didn't back down. "That's why you ate that chicken. You didn't want to see what they were going to do to him!"

"Shut up, shut up, shut up!" Lucinda clamped her hands over her ears.

"Where is he?" Noah grabbed Lucinda's arms and shook her.

Lucinda slumped against Noah as if she needed to lean on her for comfort, but the next instant she was upright again with a knife in her hand. She whirled Noah around and pulled her close, holding the knife against her throat. The quickness of it and her crazed eyes froze me into place. She put her mouth close to Noah's ear. "Never expected that I'd use your own knife against you. You really shouldn't be carrying any weapons. You'd never have the stomach to use them."

"Luce, what are you doing?" Noah was still calm, but fear laced the words. "We're friends!"

"We were *never* friends. The Hunters are right. We're nothing but animals to you guys. The only way the world will be safe is if there are no more Unbounded."

"Including Patrick?" Seconds clicked by in my mind. Each one that passed meant an increasing chance that Patrick would be killed, if he hadn't been already. But we couldn't abandon Noah to Lucinda, not if there was any chance she'd end up captured by either the Hunters or the Emporium. Since no hospital employees or security had yet come to investigate our very loud exchange, it wasn't likely their officers would be any help. I would have shifted to Lucinda then, but Keene's hand on my arm stopped me. His face was drawn as he stared at something past me down the hall. I risked a quick glance behind but saw no one.

"Please," Noah said to Lucinda, "I don't want you to get hurt."

I'd started wondering why Noah didn't try to free herself from Lucinda, who still had to be feeling the effects of the poison. Noah wasn't great at fighting, but she was trained, and we'd certainly jump in to help. Guess that was my answer—she really did love Lucinda.

"I don't care what happens to me," Lucinda cried. "Patrick's different now!"

I shrugged off Keene's hand and inched closer. This hospital was large and she had information that I was going to get from her one way or another. "He's who he's supposed to be."

"No! He's not!"

"Changing doesn't mean you become someone else," I said. "It's like growing up or learning a new language. Inside, Patrick's still who he always was. He still loves you."

"That's right!" Noah jumped in. "He still likes Mexican restaurants and long walks on the beach. He still hiccups funny. He buys you flowers and remembers your special dates. He knows you hate chocolate but will eat anything with salt. He's the same man."

"No, no," moaned Lucinda. "He's different. He's stronger, more confident. Not afraid of anything." Her voice began to rise with each point. "He doesn't get sick. He barely needs sleep. He doesn't age. He can do a dozen things with his mind at the same time." She was nearly screaming now. "He never forgets anything because he files it away and can access it with that stupid neural transmitter. So don't tell me he's the same. He's not! And he's still changing. The Hunters are right. He'll become a monster just like the one who murdered my baby and destroyed my life."

"He won't!" Noah twisted her neck, struggling to look at Lucinda, unheeding of the knife at her throat.

"Not Patrick. He's one of the good guys! All those changes you talk about are good ones. You *know* him. He's a good man. He's sacrificed his own goals to help the world. How can you say he'll become a monster?"

Lucinda's face hardened, becoming something ugly. "He sacrificed us too. Always in the limelight. Always the stares." Her attention flicked past us down the hall.

Keene followed her eyes. "Is that where they have Patrick?"

"Don't move!" Lucinda ordered, her voice no longer moaning or uncertain. "Or I'll hurt Noah. I swear it. She's so thin, so fragile, much weaker than the agent I killed at the house. All those self-defense classes Patrick made me take, you know. I may be weak from the poison, but I promise, I can stop her long enough for the Hunters to get her. After they're finished with Patrick."

"You mean, after they cut him into three pieces." Keene took a step toward her, his face a mask of fury.

I thought Keene would jump at her then, but he leaned close to me, his words coming so faint I had to strain to hear. "There's something odd about one of the doors near the end of the hall. Some kind of energy. Patrick might be there." I hoped he was right. Because if they'd left the hospital altogether while Lucinda distracted us, we might never catch up to them in time.

"Go see!" I said to him.

"Stop!" Lucinda shouted as Keene started to turn. "I'm. Saving. Humanity!" With each word she pushed the knife deeper into Noah's neck, perhaps intent on cutting out her gift of music. Blood sprang up around the blade. Keene hesitated. "Hunters are the only way we'll survive!" Lucinda continued. "If Patrick was his old self, he'd agree this was the only way."

"You're wrong. Patrick knows he's the only hope we have of uniting humanity before the Emporium takes control. The president needs him to help pass laws that will protect everyone." I glanced at Keene, brushing my hand against his so he'd know what I intended. We needed to end this now. His head dipped a fraction. Letting my knife slip into my left hand, I reached for the numbers, and sluggishly they obeyed.

"Well, *everyone* can't have him." Lucinda shook Noah. "*She* can't have him! This Unbounded slut is just like all those women with the signs, wanting his favors, offering the baby I can't give him. I *won't* let any of you have him! He's mine!" With a fluid motion, she raked the knife over Noah's throat. Blood gushed down into the front of Noah's dress. Noah cried out, but the wound apparently wasn't fatal—not even temporarily so—and Noah remained on her feet.

Anger fueling my energy, I shifted, appearing behind Lucinda. My bad arm slid around her waist to hold her in place, a bite of pain stealing my breath. My knife pierced her clothing near her left kidney. "Let her go or I'll put this inside you." I kept my voice light but pushed the point of the knife into her flesh, letting the metal speak for me. I could smell the sour stench of her body, vomit mixed with expensive perfume. I could also feel her fear because she was shaking with it. There was something intimate about the moment; I understood her as I wouldn't if I'd simply pointed a gun at her head. My knife begged to go deeper.

"Oh, I get it," Lucinda said, mocking now. "You're not Homeland Security, are you? You're one of *them*." She looked around at me, her blue eyes as pale and cold as ice. No wildness there now. Only calculation.

I gave an insincere chuckle. "Finally, something you got right. You know what? Maybe Patrick *is* different. Maybe like me, he's happy he's Changed. Maybe like me he feels alive for the first time in his life. Now let her go!"

Lucinda loosened her hold, and Noah nearly fell from her grip. Sighing, Noah leaned against the wall, her hand going to her neck, her breath ragged.

I stepped even closer to Lucinda until our bodies touched, still keeping the knife in place. Lucinda betraying Patrick hurt me in ways I didn't know I could still feel about Trevor. "You may think you're Patrick's one great love, but you know what? Next year you're going to be nothing more than the woman who betrayed him to a murderous cult, the unhinged woman he wished he'd never met. I know because that's all my dead husband is to me now—eyes I can barely remember, a pretty face I wish I hadn't wasted time on."

"Mari," Keene said. His synergy crackled through the air, an offer of help if I needed it. Or perhaps a warning.

I released her. "Right. Let's find Patrick." I started down the hall.

"Monster!" With a cry, Lucinda raised her knife and plunged it toward my back, but Noah was there, pushing me out of the way.

The knife sliced deeply through the flesh and muscle of Noah's shoulder. That should have been it, but instead of stopping there, the blade continued on with force, down in an arc until it embedded in Lucinda's own stomach. She gasped and pulled out the knife. Let it clatter to the floor.

For an instant no one moved. An agonizing second filled with horror and realization. Then both women collapsed, the back of Lucinda's head slamming sickeningly on the tile. Keene caught Noah before hers did the same. His face was devoid of color, and I could no longer feel his synergy. I knew that meant he'd used his ability on Lucinda, to enhance her strength after she'd plunged the knife through Noah's shoulder. Otherwise, she might have stopped her thrust in time to save herself.

What's more, I knew he'd done it to save me, both from being hurt and from having to hurt her. He might not have meant to give her quite that much energy, but he'd chosen to use his ability, and now he'd have to live with it.

"Is she . . . ?" he asked.

"I don't know." Lucinda was bleeding badly, but I was more concerned about Noah. Not because she wouldn't heal, but because she was more vulnerable now to whatever group was here at the hospital.

Keene removed his shirt and balled it against Lucinda's

stomach, placing her hands over it. Her eyelids fluttered but she remained unconscious.

"Go get Patrick," Noah said as I knelt beside her. Her voice sounded odd, whistling and wet. Air bubbled the blood welling from her throat, and looking at it twisted my insides, reminding me of Trevor.

I dragged my eyes away and nodded at Keene. "You go. I'll stay with her. They might have someone watching the monitors." I removed my own jacket, exposing my bare arms and arm sheaths, and began tying it awkwardly around Noah's hurt shoulder and under the opposite arm to stem the copious flow of blood.

"I'll be back." Keene turned and sprinted down the hall, his face angry and determined.

"Go with him." Noah's dark eyes pleaded. "If Hunters or the Emporium were coming, they'd already be here. It's Patrick they're after, not me."

I debated only a few seconds. "Okay, but text Jace, if you can. Let him know what's happening." I put Noah's phone into her right hand and placed her gun on the floor next to her, removing the silencer. "Use the gun if anyone comes. I'll hear and shift back to help you."

She nodded. "Just find him."

CHAPTER 17

I SHIFTED NEXT TO KEENE, WHO'D STOPPED AT A DOOR JUST before the yellow caution tape where the hallway intersected another that ran both left and right. Peering around the corner, I saw a nurses' station far down the hall where three women seemed to be at work. A man with an untrimmed beard sat behind them, awkwardly dressed as a doctor, one hand hidden by another white smock puddled in his lap. Definitely not Emporium.

"Hunter," I whispered.

"Something's strange here." Keene had his hand flat on the door.

He was right. When I tried to call up numbers that would get me into the room, nothing came. There were simply no coordinates available except maybe a foot or so beyond the door. "Definitely, something's blocking me. There's a tiny bit of space. I might be able to shift just to the other side."

"We have no idea what's there." Keene tried the knob and found it locked. "We'll go in the old-fashioned way."

"Why don't we just knock? Don't they have a special pattern?"

"Yeah, but my info will be way out of date, especially if an Emporium agent has infiltrated their group. They'll have changed protocol."

"Try it anyway."

He gave a series of taps that sounded rather juvenile instead of cool. We waited, hearing low murmurs. Footsteps, and then the doorknob turned.

Keene shoved hard on the door before it opened more than a few inches. As he pushed inside, two men pounced on him. He threw them back, knocking one down with a punch and pistol-whipping the hand of the one who held a gun. I sprinted past them all, seeing that Keene had it under control. He didn't move as fast as Jace, but every punch was carefully placed and accelerated by his synergy. I was pretty sure the first man he'd hit wouldn't be getting up again, but the other, dressed in the jeans and T-shirt that were typical Hunter garb, moved like a combat Unbounded. He had to be an Emporium plant.

The part of the room I could see was empty except for a few beds and several odd, three-foot metal poles emitting streams of yellow light that intersected one another. The far part of the room was curtained, and the lights from these transmitters continued through this curtained area, the plastic-backed material was pulled slightly aside for that purpose. The instant I passed through the light stream in front of the doorway, I could feel Patrick's color and calculate the numbers that would take me to him.

Clicking the release on my left arm sheath to slide the knife into my hand, I shifted across the room and past the curtain. On the other side, it looked as if a tornado had ripped through the place. Overturned chairs, scattered medical instruments, and red trash cans with DANGER printed on them spilled everywhere. Blinds had been pulled from the window and several machines smashed. Papers, needles, and wrappers mixed in with tongue depressors and alcohol wipes. The single bed had been pushed up against the wall and in it was Patrick, cuts and bruises on his face, his eyes filled with terror. His hands and legs were secured to the bed with silver duct tape, his mouth had a swath over it, and more tape layered his chest and secured him to the bed. Evidently he'd fought hard.

A tall, thin man in green scrubs stood over him, a needle in hand. On a tiny table next to him was a large saw that was stained dark with old blood. *Definitely a Hunter,* I thought. No doubt about what he'd been intending, though usually Hunters didn't sedate their victims, believing that the suffering freed their souls from their vile natures.

The man was staring blankly at the curtain when I appeared, obviously worried by the racket Keene and his opponent were making. His face was closely shaven, except for the droopy brown moustache. His untrimmed eyebrows resembled caterpillars marching across his ruddy brow. When he saw my knife, his face paled.

Patrick also saw me and renewed his struggle, the panic fading from his face. The Hunter looked between me and his needle. I could almost see his brain working. Then, thrusting his jaw forward, he dived at Patrick, who jerked up, bashing his forehead into the side of the Hunter's skull. The man stumbled backward.

Go, Patrick!

I reached for numbers, intending to shift behind the Hunter, but a sudden dizziness prevented my fold. The second time I got it right. The Hunter whirled on me as I appeared, the needle aimed at my eye. Instinctively, I brought my wounded right arm up to block. His arm crashed into mine. For an instant, my vision went red with agony as something ripped inside my arm.

But the knife in my left hand found its way to his body.

He screamed.

So easy, it would be to slip it farther up, to pierce his lungs. Then a mere twist into his heart and he'd never kill another Unbounded again. The music of the knife beckoned. He deserved it. He'd been going to murder Patrick.

I fought to step back from my desire for revenge. Wasn't he a victim of his own lack of education? A pawn of the Emporium and other men who used their fervency to further their own agendas? But I didn't really buy that because all the Hunters I'd met seemed to use their belief as an excuse for murder—the most heinous, horrific kind of murder. No, there was nothing redeeming about this man. Nothing to hold back my hungry knife.

Nothing except my stronger desire not to be like him.

"Mari!" Keene swept open the curtain, his gun aimed at the Hunter. "It's over. You don't have to."

I let out a sudden breath, then dragged more air into my lungs. Painfully, as if it'd been far too long since I had taken a breath. I stepped back, my entire body shaking, and Keene rushed forward to deal with the Hunter.

Moments later, I was trying to pull tape from Patrick's mouth when the door slammed open to reveal Cort and Jace with Noah between them. "Patrick!" Noah rushed forward and would have fallen if Jace hadn't caught her. "Oh, thank, God!" With her good hand, she pulled the knife from my grasp and began working at the tape holding Patrick's arms. After making sure Noah wasn't going to collapse or cut herself, Jace drew out another knife and freed Patrick's legs.

Patrick sat up and hugged Noah. "Luce?" he asked.

Noah's smile fled. "I'm sorry Patrick. She didn't make it. A nurse is with her now."

Pain filled Patrick's face. "Did the Hunters . . ."

"No!" My voice came out a little too forcefully. "It was her, Patrick. She's responsible for her own death. She was behind everything. Those texts on the way here? She betrayed you to the Hunters. She tried to kill Noah."

Patrick wilted and tears started down his face. He reached out a hand, stopping short of the deep gash on

Noah's neck. The bleeding had mostly stopped, but it still looked terrible. "Luce did all that?" he said. "I didn't know she had it in her." Was that admiration in his voice? He must really love her. "I'm so sorry, Noah." His hands dropped to hers and clung tightly. "Why couldn't Luce trust me?"

Noah leaned her forehead to rest against his. "I don't know. Maybe she just never recovered from what the Emporium did to her. Maybe she had a problem separating you from that bastard who killed her child. But you're doing the right thing. The only thing."

I hated that Noah could still give Lucinda excuses. After over a century and a half, Noah should know better. Except I bet Cort would say that her age was exactly why Noah spoke the way she did.

"What about everyone else?" Patrick pulled away from Noah as he spoke, showing his strength and leadership in that simple question. "Susan? Chance? The other agents?"

"Susan's the cook, right?" Jace asked. "She's fine, and it looks like all the Secret Service agents at the house will survive as well. The paramedics think that's because they were in awesome shape. We're betting there's damage, but the prognosis is good. They were giving that Secret Service agent—Chance, right?—a third bag of blood, last we heard. He's one tough sucker."

"Good." Patrick managed a strangled smile. Of course, the dead agent at his house hadn't been so lucky—Lucinda had seen to that—but no one brought it up, and I certainly wasn't going to. It could wait for another day. There was already enough guilt and heartache to go around.

Keene finished with the Hunter, having used the man's own duct tape to secure him on the far side of the room next to the others he'd captured. He returned to stand awkwardly by the bed. "Patrick," he said. "I'm really sorry about Lucinda. We tried . . . I didn't mean . . ."

I touched Keene's hand and gave a slight shake of my head. Now was not the time to confess his role in Lucinda's demise. He'd only been trying to save Noah and me, so we could get to Patrick, but even the noble Patrick might not see it that way right now.

"Thank you," Patrick said, his voice scarcely recognizable. "Please, I need to see her."

Noah nodded. "I'll go with you. I probably should let that nurse bandage me up anyway. She wasn't happy about me leaving. Jace gave me curequick, and I can feel I'm healing, but stitches will help."

"Wait. There's a man out there at the nurses' station," I said.

Jace shook his head. "Not anymore. We rounded up five Hunters before we got to Noah. Lucky she texted, because your GPS signals vanished before we made it up here. Had us a bit worried. We had to track her instead."

"It's their transmitters—some kind of blocking technology." I wasn't surprised to see Cort already studying one of the devices. "Doesn't seem to need wires like the one we use, but it kept me from shifting to Patrick."

"We'll take them with us." Cort switched off the one near him and picked it up. "Hmm, surprisingly heavy. Definitely new technology, but if they aren't in sight of one another, or if something steps in the way, they can't work. Still, they have their uses."

Yeah, I thought, *like today.*

Patrick's pants were buzzing, and in a daze he pulled his phone from his pocket. He stared through the cracked glass at a message. "Looks like my dad's gotten wind of this. He wants to know if I'm okay." He handed the phone to Noah. "I really can't deal with that right now." With effort, he swung his feet off the bed and stood.

"That means Secret Service is about to descend on us." Cort handed the blocking device to Jace. "Go with Patrick and Noah just in case we have any stray Hunters out there. But grab a few of these on your way out and stash them someplace. I don't want to lose this tech to the government."

As Jace exited the room with Noah and Patrick, Keene's eyes followed them—unreadable like they'd been after the explosion in Morocco. "It's good you stopped Lucinda when you did," I said softly, "or Noah and Patrick might not have a future. And they will, you can see that, can't you? Give it a little time."

Without a word, Keene picked me up and set me on the edge of the tall bed. Carefully, he eased up the right sleeve of my blouse, where I noticed for the first time that blood had leaked through the gauze and was running down my arm. He found a pair of scissors in the mess around us and began cutting off the bandage. "Looks like you ripped out the stitches."

"I don't want any more. All I need is a good night sleep with no bad guys showing up. Can you do that for me?"

He studied me for several seconds in silence, then nodded. "Okay. For now, I'll just wrap it tight enough to hold back some of that blood." From an inner pocket, he pulled out a small vial filled with a clear substance and handed it to me before resuming his examination of my wound. I swallowed a mouthful of the sweet curequick. It was so thick, it almost made me gag.

On the other side of the room, Cort finished picking up the transmitters. He motioned to our three captives. "Jace and I'll be back for these guys in a minute. Or the police will be."

Keene nodded at his brother. "Just make sure they know the guy in the black T-shirt is a combat Unbounded. He'll need special attention."

"Ah, that explains the hog-tying. I wondered about that. The ripped sheets must mean you ran out of rope."

"I can only carry so much. I'm not Ritter."

Cort's lips twitched. "Nope. You're not quite that obsessed. Yet." It was good to see them joking, and my worry for Keene eased.

After Cort was gone, I kicked Keene's leg lightly. "Will you finish poking around there already? That hurts."

"Just need to wrap it now. Looks like the exit wound is healing nicely, and the artery must have had time to seal or you would have lost more blood and passed out already."

"I nearly did when I tried to shift to help Patrick. Took me a couple tries."

Keene's face drew in concern. "Maybe my synergy—"

"It's not you, it's me. Before when I'd shift, I'd pass through a place I call the *in between*. Cort says it's like opening a wormhole or something. Yeah, *I know*, that's so Star Trek. But now when I shift you and the others, I'm folding the new location around me instead. I don't see the *in between*. I'm not sure what that means."

Keene's hands stilled as he considered. "Different process, I'm betting. Maybe pulling takes more energy, or maybe just a different muscle."

"That's what it feels like. The *in between* is easier, so I want to try moving us that way."

"Now?"

I groaned. "Right now I don't think I could shift two inches." Actually, the curequick had begun to work, and I felt as if several jolts of caffeine had entered my system, so maybe before long I would be ready.

Cort and Jace returned with several police officers to round up the Hunters and the Emporium plant. A buzz from the hallway spilled in after them. "This place is hopping with what must be every officer and agent in Washington DC," Jace announced with a happy grin.

"Just don't get your picture taken," Keene warned.

Cort laughed. "No worries, the president is with Patrick now, and they're keeping the media at bay. We'll be ready to leave in a few minutes. We just want to make sure they get these guys properly secured."

Keene finished wrapping my arm with gauze, and we watched them haul away the prisoners. Once we were alone, the ensuing silence was almost more than I could stand. I eyed the pillow that had at some point fallen from the bed, wishing I could lie down and take a nice long nap—in Keene's arms.

"So," he said, his voice low. "You said Patrick and Noah have a future. What about us? Is that what we have? A future?"

I didn't hesitate because I couldn't imagine a life that didn't include him. "Yes. But . . ."

"But what?" His expression turned solemn.

"It *does* make a difference, you being Unbounded." Before he could misunderstand, I rushed on, "Mortals, they're so . . . I mean, look at Patrick. Look at Stella."

I was trying to say that I'd still want him if he were mortal, but that didn't mean I was eager to experience the heartache I'd witnessed when Stella lost her first husband—and would experience again if she pursued her relationship with Chris.

"You being Unbounded," I said, making another attempt, "is so much . . . easier."

Keene's head tilted as he regarded me for several heart-beats. His voice, when it came, felt like a promise. "Then that's a good thing."

He kissed me then, and energy thickened around us. Numbers swirled, painting the world with colors I'd never seen in such variety. His synergy increased every-thing in me, even the intensity of his touch.

I could *so* get used to this. And I'd have time to.

Exhilaration filled me. Still sitting on the bed, I wrapped my legs around him, pulling him closer until our bodies met. My heart sounded like a drum in my ears, a pounding, furious beat that pumped my veins full of anticipation.

The sensation blotted out all the horrors we'd expe-rienced, past and present, and even the beckoning siren call of my knives, the worry I had of giving into them. Of becoming what the Hunters' fear had tried to make me. I was a Renegade, a Guardian of Humanity. I wasn't a monster. I'd *never* become the monster Lucinda had accused me of being.

We broke apart as the others returned to the room, Patrick leading the way, his face rigid, his eyes red with mourning. His bruises were much blacker now as they began to heal, but determination exuded from his eyes.

"I think I'm ready to leave," he said. "I've refused my father's strong suggestion that I continue with the Secret Service, so I'm hoping you'll all stay with me until the laws he's trying to pass become a reality. I have a lot more work to do with the American people to bring about the peace we're searching for."

I looked around at Keene, Cort, and Jace before answering for everyone. "Of course, we will. That's why we're here."

"I'm staying too," said a newly bandaged Noah. "I have a few performances I'll have to do, but besides that, I'm free."

Patrick nodded at her. "I'd like that." His gaze refocused on me. "However, there is the little matter of getting out of here. It's a circus out there. I don't know about you guys, but after today, I could use a good night's sleep somewhere without any media or agents or snipers."

I slid down from the bed. "We were just talking about that. With Keene's help, I can probably shift you out of here."

"Just you," Keene added. "If we give her another half hour to recoup her strength. The others will have to meet us."

"Aw," Jace said. "Just when I was looking forward to hurtling through space again."

I laughed. "Maybe later."

"I know a place we can go." Noah stepped to a chair and sat down. Her very dark skin didn't look paler, but it was obvious she was feeling faint by the way she moved. "One of my properties has room for all of us. Complete with the latest in Renegade security. We tried the mortal way with Secret Service, now let's do it Unbounded style. With Mari's help, no one will ever know you're there. You can stay as long as you like."

Patrick gave a sigh. "That sounds good. Is there room for my cook? Susan's been through a lot today, and I'd like her to be safe too."

"Absolutely."

"I'll have to shift somewhere I know," I reminded them. "We'll go to Noah's by car from there. At least this first time."

"Okay. We'll meet you back where we've been staying." Cort offered Noah an arm. She smiled at him and then at Jace as he offered his arm as well.

"Be careful," Patrick cautioned.

Noah let go of Cort and Jace long enough to hug him goodbye. "We'll be fine." That didn't stop Patrick from frowning as the door closed behind them. I understood his worry. He'd lost so much today.

"I think I'm ready now," I said.

"You sure?" Keene asked.

I loved the way he seemed to peer into the depths of my soul, unafraid of what he might find there. When I responded, it wasn't really to the question he'd asked, but to the unasked one lurking in those eyes. "I'm absolutely sure."

His energy gathered, stealing my breath as every bit as sensuously as his kiss had earlier. I called up the coordinates that would lead us to our destination, but hovering ever nearby were those other coordinates in Venezuela.

Soon, I told myself. Keene would be in for a surprise.

For now, I concentrated on using the *in between* instead of folding the location around us, hoping it would be easier. As I reached for Keene's hand to begin the shift, my eyes snagged on the merest corner of the plastic bacon poking out of the gauze covering my wound.

Laughter bubbled up inside me. I wasn't sure yet how to top that. But I would.

THE END

TEYLA BRANTON GREW UP AVIDLY READING SCIENCE FICTION AND fantasy and watching Star Trek reruns with her large family. They lived on a little farm where she loved to visit the solitary cow and collect (and juggle) the eggs, usually making it back to the house with most of them intact. On that same farm she once owned thirty-three gerbils and eighteen cats, not a good mix, as it turns out. Teyla always had her nose in a book and daydreamed about someday creating her own worlds.

Teyla is now married, mostly grown up, and has seven kids, including a three-year-old, so life at her house can be very interesting (and loud), but writing keeps her sane. She thrives on the energy and daily amusement offered by her children, the semi-ordered chaos giving her a constant source of writing material. Grabbing any snatch of free time from her hectic life, Teyla writes novels, often with a child on her lap. She warns her children that if they don't behave, they just might find themselves in her next book!

She's been known to wear pajamas all day when working on a deadline, and is often distracted enough to burn dinner. (Okay, pretty much 90% of the time.) A sign on her office door reads: DANGER. WRITER AT WORK. ENTER AT YOUR OWN RISK.

She loves writing fiction and traveling, and she hopes to write and travel a lot more. She also loves shooting guns, martial arts, and belly dancing. She has worked in the publishing business for over twenty years. Teyla also writes romance and suspense under the name Rachel Branton. For more information, please visit http://www.TeylaBranton.com.

CPSIA information can be obtained
at www.ICGtesting.com
Printed in the USA
LVOW01s2144261115

464290LV00013B/185/P